BETRAYAL AT STONEHENGE - 1000 B.C.

BETRAYAL AT STONEHENGE - 1000 B.C.

By

James Nesper

Illustrations by Vern Beyer

ISBN: 978-1-5872-1071-6 (sc)

1stBooks - rev. 5/16/01

ABOUT THE BOOK

Stonehenge is just too fascinating to ignore. The word "Stonehenge" seems to ignite the imagination of people and arouse their curiosity.

That is because the accomplishments of the valiant Stonehenge people are incredible. It is believed that 123 large blue colored stones were quarried, cut to specified rectangular shapes and transported from the Preseli Mountains in Wales. This is a distance of approximately 130 miles as the crow flies and 240 miles when rafting the stones at sea, navigating several rivers upstream and portaging from one river to another. Eighty-two stone uprights weighing up to seven tons and forty-one top stones weighing slightly less were transported. Such an enormous undertaking seems like an impossible task for illiterate prehistoric people, but they did it. The stones are there to prove it.

Approximately 1000 years later even greater construction was begun. The five towering rectangular trilithons stones (or archways), arranged in the shape of a horseshoe and facing the direction of the summer solstice, were built. At least 56 other huge stones were brought to Stonehenge probably from Marlborough Downs over 20 miles away. The largest stone weighed 55 tons and the average weighed 26 tons. It is difficult to imagine how stones of such bulk could be cut to size and transported before the practical use of the wheel, modern roads, hydraulic machinery, wire or nylon rope, etc. Moreover, the horses of that time were small, more like the modern Exmore pony, and were not used as beasts of burden.

Once the stones were transported, they had to be positioned to allow for twelve perfect astronomical alignments and the heavy lintels had to be raised to the tops of the pillars presumably by backbreaking human labor.

So who were these amazing people who built Stonehenge? How did they do it, and why? *Betrayal at Stonehenge—1000 B.C.* breathes life into the people, puts flesh and blood on their skeletal remains and creates saints and sinners. It takes place at the mysterious fall of Stonehenge, around 1000 B.C. Murder, lust, loyalty and love are combined with summer solstice and eclipse of the sun and their mystical religious settings. The genre is late bronze age but the setting is definitely STONEHENGE.

THE INTRODUCTION

"Stonehenge is the most famous prehistoric monument in the entire world. In fact it is ranked with the great pyramids of Egypt as the most famous monument that the ancient world has given us." By Dr. Ronald Hutton PhD. , University of Bristol, England.

Many people have an intelligent curiosity about the famous Stonehenge monument. They are amazed at the industry and knowledge of prehistoric people who built it and who worshiped there. After thousands of years there are only educated guesses as to the purpose of the structure and how it was built. In this age of computers and telecommunication, they are surprised to learn that the builders accomplished so much with no apparent written language. (1)

Books, articles and academic research material have been written about Stonehenge in every translatable language. Roman conquerors, clerics of all stripes, experts commissioned by kings and prime ministers, engineers, astronomers, historians, scholars, anthropologists, archaeologists and an army of curious and informed private citizens have examined the mysteries of Stonehenge for the past 2,000 years. Yet, assumptions concerning how and why it was built remain conjectural, hypothetical and sometimes purely speculative. In short, Stonehenge remains a sequence of delightful enigmas that titillate the reader compelling him to learn more. (2)

EARLY STONEHENGE How far back into the unfathomed past does the history of Stonehenge go? No one really knows and one can only guess. The fact that the soil under sections of Stonehenge has never been plowed for farming creates many questions. Is this the same virgin soil deposited eons ago when the British Isles were separated from the European continent? Stonehenge is surrounded by the Salisbury Plain which was farmed before records were kept. From what we know about prehistoric agriculture, farmers would till a section of land until the soil was totally exhausted, then move on to another section. Why was Stonehenge not farmed for thousands of years when all the land in the immediate proximity was farmed extensively? Was this area considered sacred by the hunter-food gatherers before farming began, and why did subsequent generations continue to respect and protect this site? (3)

Establishing any dates at Stonehenge was an educated guess until the development of the radio carbon dating technique. Two post-holes where giant pine posts had been placed were found in the parking lot adjacent to Stonehenge. Post-hole B is pegged at roughly 7100 B.C. and Post-hole A is a thousand years older at 8100 B.C. It is safe to say that Stonehenge was the focus of some kind of ceremonial and possibly astronomical activity nine or ten thousand years ago. (3)

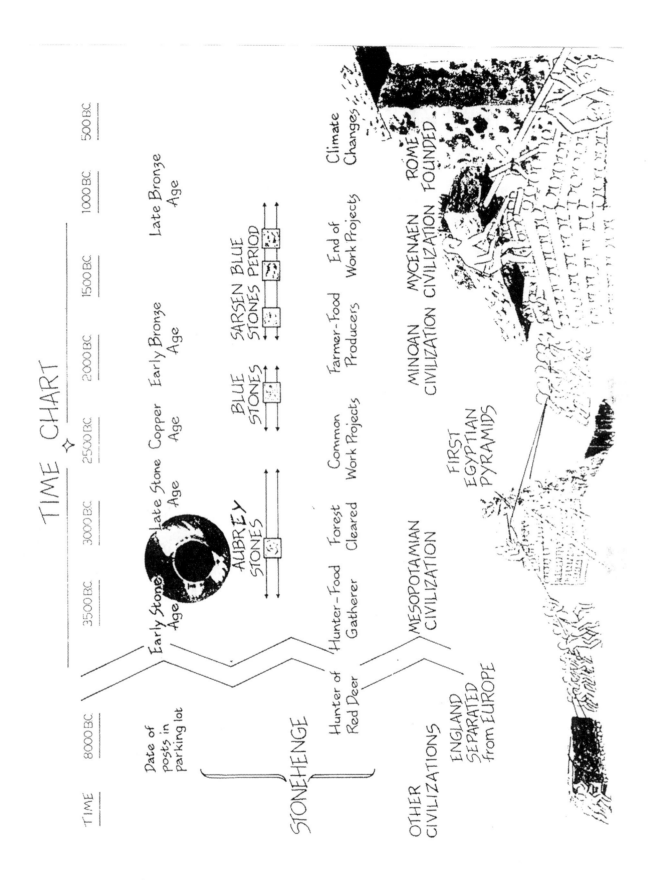

TIME CHART

TIME	8000 BC	3500 BC	3000 BC	2500 BC	2000 BC	1500 BC	1000 BC	500 BC

Date of posts in parking lot

Early Stone Age · Late Stone Age · Copper Age · Early Bronze Age · Late Bronze Age

AUBREY STONES · BLUE STONES · SARSEN BLUE STONES PERIOD

STONEHENGE

Hunter-Food Gatherer · Forest Cleared · Common Work Projects · Farmer-Food Producers · End of Work Projects

Hunter of Red Deer

OTHER CIVILIZATIONS

MESOPOTAMIAN CIVILIZATION

ENGLAND SEPARATED from EUROPE

FIRST EGYPTIAN PYRAMIDS

MINOAN CIVILIZATION · MYCENAEN CIVILIZATION · ROME FOUNDED

Climate Changes

The site of Stonehenge does not have a commanding presence high on top of a mount like many great cathedrals. To the west the ground rises slightly while the ground falls away gradually in all other directions. The monument is built on a slight hillside which was not the best site by any standard. Why? What was so important about this specific piece of real estate? We don't know the answer to any of these questions, but I will write more about the location of Stonehenge under "station stones."

RING RELIGION PERIOD   It is possible that Stonehenge was only an earthen ditch and embankment for first 6000 years.   On the outer perimeter of Stonehenge there is a circular ditch approximately 20 feet wide with varying depths, and inside the ditch there is an earth embankment which is approximately 2 feet high with a mean diameter of 320 feet. This suggests that Stonehenge was part of the ancient ring religion of Great Britain. Some of these ring ditches and mounds have been dated to 5000 B.C. or 1000 years before the great civilizations of Egypt and the Middle East. There are still approximately 600 ring ditches scattered about Great Britain today, but none is as significant and well known as Stonehenge. (4)

True circular rings are believed to have been made by tying a leather cord around a stake fixed in the ground. It was stretched out to the desired radius and a circle could be inscribed. Then a ditch could be dug, earth embankments created and/or the stones positioned. (5)

The specific purpose of the ring ditches is not clear and may be lost in antiquity. The circular interior of the ring ditches may have been used in the burial rite, but apparently only seldom as the actual burial site. They may have been used as a monument to the success of a regional clan chief or priest. Others may have been used as a great meeting place of the clan to market their livestock, trade at fairs, and have political-social events. Still others may have been used for religious ceremony, celestial worship and to observe significant seasonal events, as Stonehenge most certainly was. Whatever the purpose, the ring ditches are found throughout the British Isles. They are found in the northern Orkney Islands off Scotland and near Land's End England over 600 miles to the south. (6)

The many ring ditches are mute testimony that there was communication and trade between the early-Stonehenge people. There appears to have been a common religion as evidenced by the circular formations and common celestial interest. There are circular ditches that closely resemble each other but they are miles apart. Professor Alexander Thom, Emeritus Professor of Engineering Science at Oxford, has proposed the Megalithic Yard, or approximately 0.829 meters, as a common unit of measure used by the builders. He has further demonstrated that the prehistoric Britons had a practical knowledge of geometry in laying out their circles. Flint could be made into excellent tools and weapons and was found hundred of miles from the mine sources, suggesting trade between the clans. Pottery and salt were also traded among the early Stonehenge people. (7)

Trading and communication probably took place in one of two ways. The clans could have traded with neighboring clans in a simple friendly exchange among the chiefs. There is little evidence of wars among the Stonehenge people, and trading might have been similar to the potlatch type of trading done by the Indians on the northwestern Pacific coast of the United States. Or trading might have developed through a person, family or clan who became professional traders. They might have become expert potters or flint knappers and could trade their superior wares. In the time of the use of copper and bronze they might have become skilled coppersmiths, bronzesmiths or even goldsmiths and traded with the nearby clans.

In my novel I assumed that the Stonehenge people did trade and therefore had a reasonably fluent understandable form of oral communication. My characters do not "grunt" and "groan" as they do in some novels of the prehistoric genre. Instead they communicated in words, as research into this time period would indicate.

The worshipers at Stonehenge were intoxicated with their own vision of the universe and their place in it. Stonehenge can only be understood when one views the broader picture of the world around it. Even today the Salisbury Plain area adjacent to Stonehenge is populated with the remains of many ancient stones, earthen ring shrines, earthen burial mounds called barrows and miles of parallel ditches called Curcuses and Avenues and others.

AVEBURY One spectacular shrine in the Salisbury Plain area close to Stonehenge is Avebury. It is larger and believed to be older than Stonehenge and made with the simplest tools of bone and leather. The two sights also illustrate two important general characteristics of the culture: the large-scale and selfconfident view of man's relationship with nature and the almost manic tenacity of a people gripped by an obsession. Even today approaching Avebury from the Kennet River on the south one experiences many architectural and landscaping devices with theatrical effects that seduce the viewer into thinking the shrine is much smaller than it is. The nine meter high and 20 meter wide earthen wall around Avebury conceals the stone circles on the inside. Entering Avebury one immediately is aware of a circular ditch twelve meters deep next to the earthen wall. Then you are overwhelmed by the two huge portal stones flanking the entrance. One is diamond shaped and weighs an estimated 60 tons. Its fallen partner was approximately 5 meters tall, 3.5 meters broad and 2 meters thick. This monster weighs approximately 90 tons which is almost twice the weight of the largest stone at Stonehenge and the most enormous stone used in any British monument. (8)

The inner courtyard is enormous, 110,000 square meters or the equivalent of over 18 football fields. Inside there are two smaller stone circles called the northern circle and a private shrine stone circle. Around the outer perimeter of the inner court is a gigantic stone circle some 427 meters in diameter consisting of 99 large upright stones. Each stone has been specially prepared with a finished surface on the inner side and a rough surface on the outer side. The coarse gnarled outer surface apparently had more of a spiritual meaning than an artistic meaning to the Stonehenge person. It may have represented man's propinquity with the earth goddess or sun goddess, a meaning which could only be truly felt by the Stonehenge people. The finished inner side possibly had a forgotten talismanic meaning as well.

STONES ARE BROUGHT TO STONEHENGE Stonehenge, Avebury and all the stone monuments near Stonehenge were not built according to specific blueprints and within a short time span like modern skyscrapers are today. They were constructed like the great cathedrals of Europe where the building took many years, even centuries, and involved many changes. The story revealed in the changes provides insight into the conflict of basic religious doctrine, perhaps disagreement between the moon and the sun worshipers, or changes in the power structure of the elite. The forgotten people who made these changes are the stuff that makes interesting, creative and exciting fiction writing.

THE AUBREY STONES [c. 3000 to c. 2150 B.C.] The antler of the red deer was used as a pick-like tool by prehistoric man. Recently such an antler was uncovered from the earth bank at Stonehenge and carbon dated to 2800 B.C. (plus or minus 200 years). Did a careless workman 4800 years ago provide the clue to the introduction of stones at Stonehenge? (9)   Stonehenge was a place of worship for approximately 500 years beginning around 3000 B.C. The site was then apparently abandoned and Stonehenge was overgrown with trees and brushes for the next 200 years. Around 2500 B.C. another group of worshipers returned to Stonehenge and built a circle of 56 stones in the inner court, and then, after a brief period of time, the stones were removed. Approximately 4100 years later, in 1660, John Aubrey discovered the ring of holes where the stones had been placed. These holes are now called the Aubrey Stones or Aubrey Holes. (10) and (11).

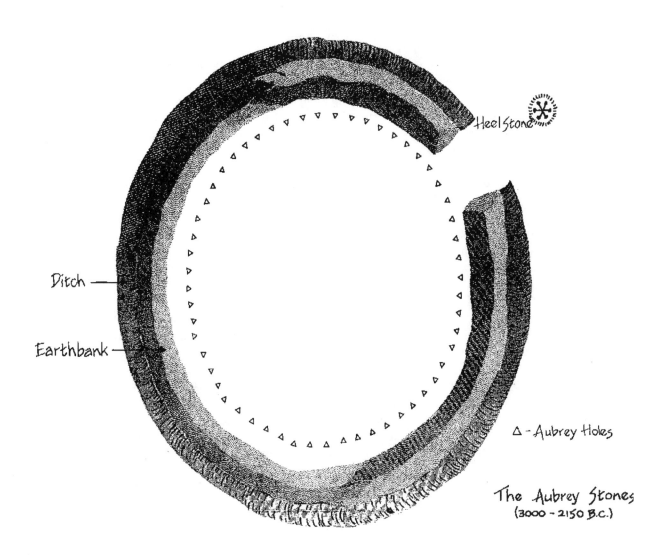

Ditch

Earthbank

Heel Stone

△ – Aubrey Holes

The Aubrey Stones
(3000 – 2150 B.C.)

Approximately 300 years later, or in 1963, it was demonstrated that the eclipse of the sun and the moon could be determined by marking positions around the Aubrey stone holes. Gerald S. Hawkins, then Professor of Astronomy at Boston University, used computerized data to unlock the mystery of the Aubrey Holes and other celestial sightings. However, like practically everything connected with Stonehenge, there are those who question his findings. (12)

THE BLUE STONES [c. 2150 to c.2000 B.C.] During this time period the four cornerstones now called the "station stones" might have been added along the edge of the earthen bank circle. The station stones could have been placed much earlier, no one knows for sure. The position of the station stones was essential to the observation of many celestial alignments which were central to the religion at that time. Even today you can sight-line eleven important sun and eleven moon positions from the station stones alignment. (12)

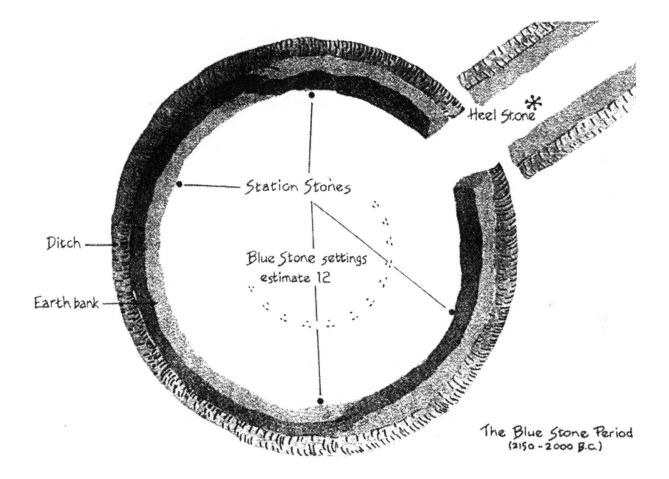

Heel Stone ∗

Station Stones

Ditch

Blue Stone settings
estimate 12

Earth bank

The Blue Stone Period
(2150 - 2000 B.C.)

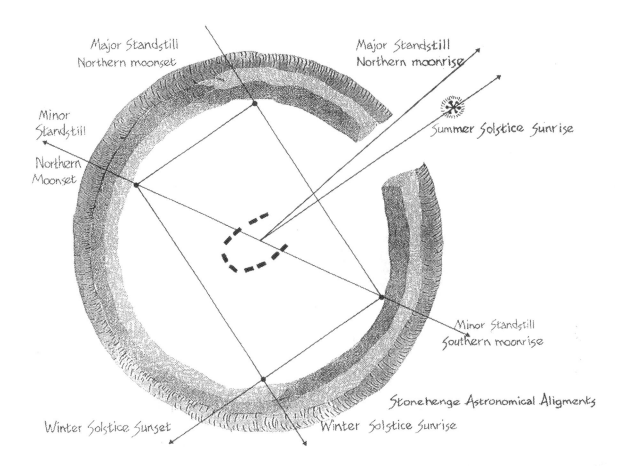

Major Standstill
Northern moonset

Major Standstill
Northern moonrise

Minor
Standstill

Summer Solstice Sunrise

Northern
Moonset

Minor Standstill
Southern moonrise

Stonehenge Astronomical Aligments

Winter Solstice Sunset

Winter Solstice Sunrise

If the station stones were located on a different site, just a few miles in a different direction, fewer celestial sightings would be seen. This was very significant to the Stonehenge people and could explain why the land was considered sacred and never plowed for farmland. The stupendous stone arches and circles that we are familiar with were built approximately six hundred years later but relied on the position of the ancient station stones for celestial sightings. (12)

The task of constructing this prehistoric shrine during this period is another enigma. It is believed that 123 large blue stones were quarried, cut to specified rectangular shapes and transported from the Preseli Mountains in Wales. This is a distance of about 130 miles, as the crow flies and 240 miles when rafting the stones at sea, navigating several rivers upstream and portaging from one river to another. Eighty-two blue stone uprights weighing up to seven tons and 41 lintel tops weighing slightly less were transported by boat and over land to Stonehenge. Such an enormous undertaking seems like an impossible task for a community of rudimental prehistoric people to accomplish, but they did, the stones are there to prove it. The presence of the stones raises questions. Why bring stones from such a distance? Why not use stones from the immediate vicinity? (13)

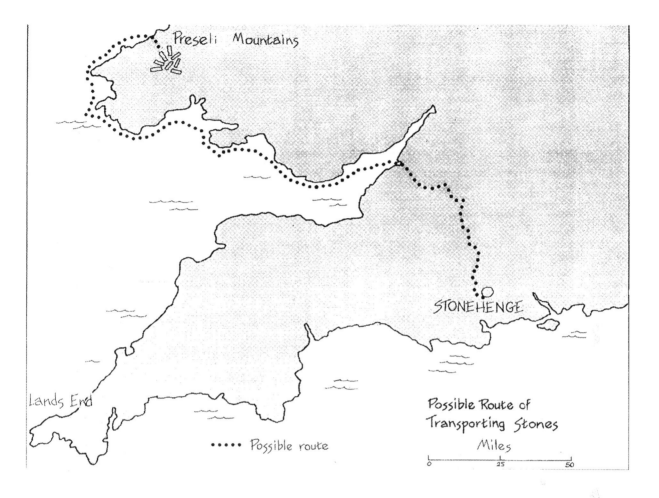

THE SARSEN STONES [c. 2000 to 1550 B.C.] This was the beginning of the greatest building period in Stonehenge's history, and ironically, it was followed by the greatest demolition period. During this period the towering boulders that we associate with Stonehenge were erected. There were five huge trilithons (or archways) arranged in the shape of a horseshoe facing the heel stone (alignment stone) and the direction of summer solstice sunrise. These archways stood 20 to 24 feet above the ground with five to eight feet buried underground and were built to last forever. Even the Roman troops could not topple them over in early AD. Large lintels were placed across the tops making massive arches. They were surrounded by a near perfect stone circle on rectangular columns 18 feet high, and lintel tops forming a continuous ring of stone. The top of the stone circle was level. To produce something level on rough stone with only crude tools was no small task.

The finding, quarrying, shaping to rectangular size, transporting and erecting the great stones represent an immense amount of time and labor. There might have been seventy-five stones shipped 20 miles from Marlborough Downs with the largest weighing 55 tons and the average weighing 26 tons. The stones, found near Avebury and Marlborough Downs, are called sarsen stone, which is a form of sandstone compressed harder than granite. It is difficult to imagine how stones of such bulk could be transported before the practical use of the wheels, modern roads, hydraulic machinery, wire or nylon rope and iron chains, etc. Moreover, the horses at that time were small, more like the modern Exmore pony, and were probably not used as beasts of burden. How were they moved? Nobody knows for sure. (14)

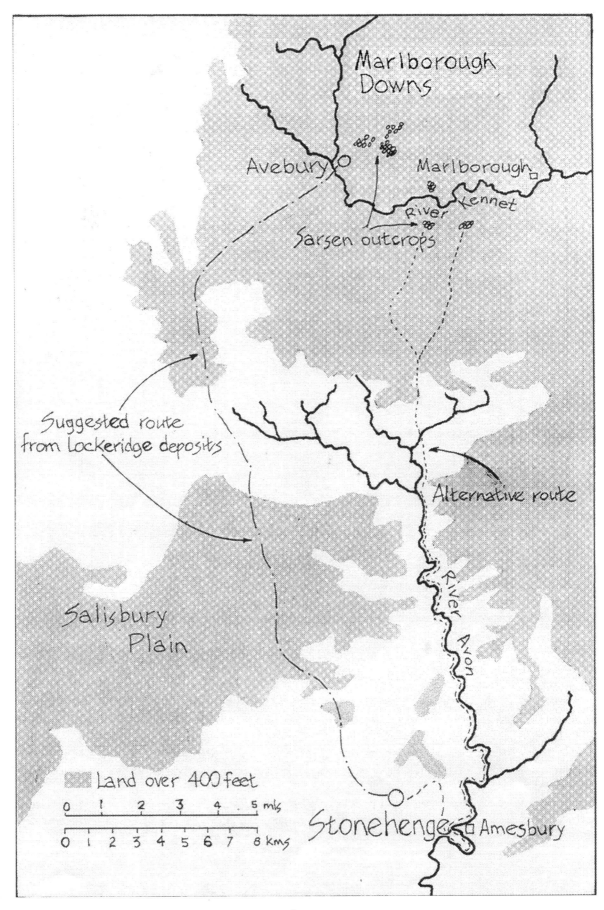

Marlborough
Downs

Avebury

Marlborough

River Kennet

Sarsen outcrops

Suggested route
from Lockeridge deposits

Alternative route

River Avon

Salisbury
Plain

Land over 400 feet

0 1 2 3 4 5 mls

0 1 2 3 4 5 6 7 8 kms

Stonehenge Amesbury

Once the stones were transported, they had to be placed in holes precisely positioned to make perfect astronomical alignments. The heavy lintels were raised to the tops of the pillars presumably by backbreaking physical labor. Between 2100 B.C. and 1550 B.C. the sarsen stones were taken down, put up again and then the whole process repeated. No concrete was used in this ambitious construction. Instead the stones were fitted together with mortise and tenon joints commonly used by carpenters in woodworking. (15)

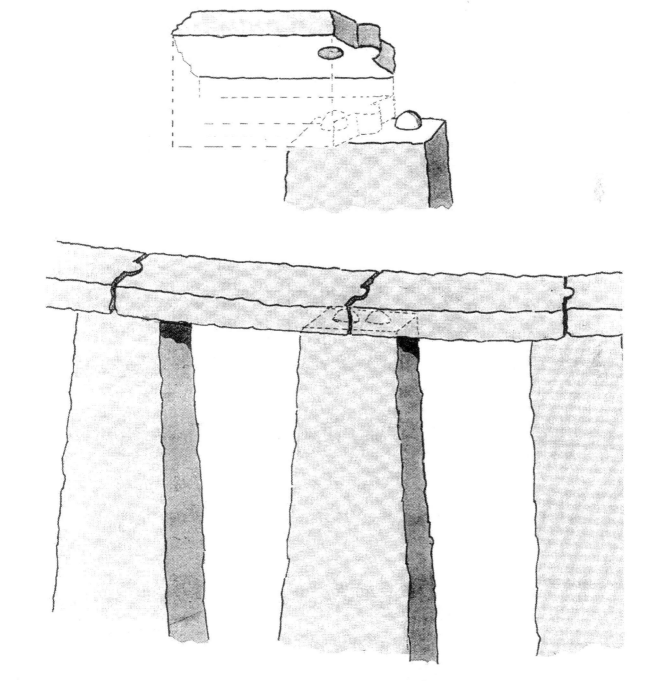

Sarsen Pillars
(Mortise and Tenon Joints)

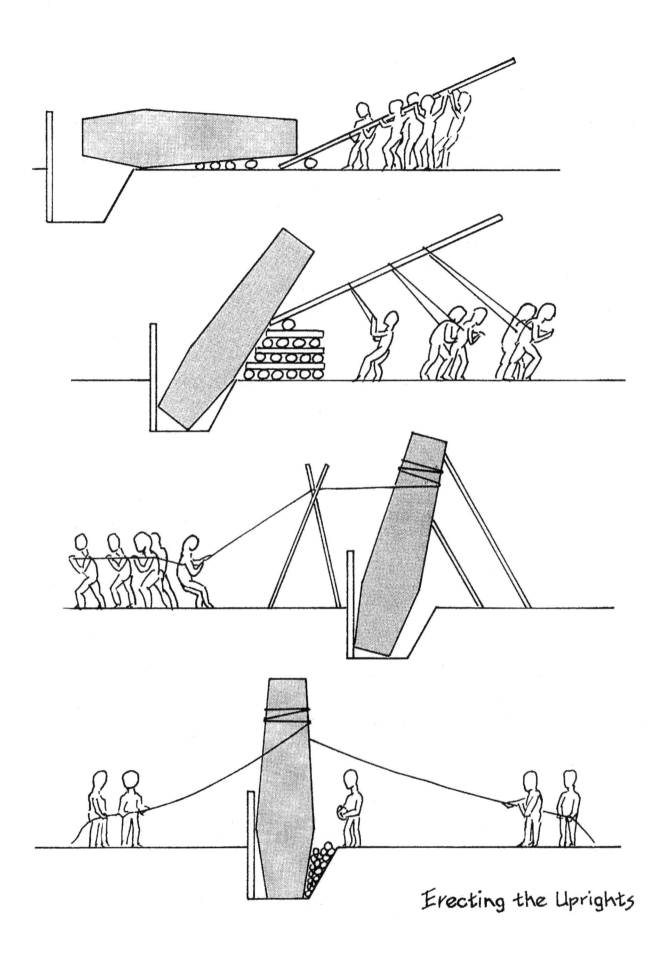

Erecting the Uprights

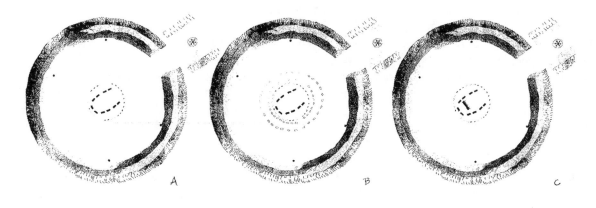

Sarsen Stone Period
(2000 – 1550 B.C.)

KEY

• Standing Stones	∴ Blue Stones	▨ Earth Bank
⁖ Stone Settings	• Station Stones	△ Aubrey Holes
○ Stone Holes	⟨⟨⟨⟨ Ditch	✳ Heel Stone

Stonehenge Phases

Later in this time period there was a similar cycle of construction with the blue stones. These stones were tooled, dressed and erected, and then, after a lapse of perhaps a hundred years, left unfinished and abandoned. Finally the dressed blue stones were erected in the circle and horseshoe formation with which we are most familiar.(16)

This seems like an extraordinary number of changes in construction, but we must realize that the time period covers approximately 1000 years or 40 generations of human development. In our modern cities we construct office buildings and apartments, tear them down and commence reconstruction of new buildings all within twenty or thirty years.

So, how was all this extensive work accomplished? This is the question that has confounded countless generations. During the Middle Ages the country folk simply believed that the task was done by Merlin, the friendly giant. Actually this is a plausible answer for the superstitious and credulous people of that time considering the herculean extent of the project. Some modern writers are just as credulous and believe that people from outer space did all the work. But humans beings did build Stonehenge with sleds, levers, manual labor and sheer determination. Estimates of the man-days of physical labor have been made by modern time and motion measuring techniques. The total man-days (eight hour work day) required is 1,497,680. This includes "carrying time" or time required to provide food, shelter and clothing to the worker. It does not include time for the organization, administration and logistics necessary for this great communal operation.

WHAT WAS THE PURPOSE OF STONEHENGE? The Stonehenge people had a love affair with the regular occurring positions of the sun and moon. The heel stone, the four station stones and others provided accurate astronomical alignments. Some of these are the summer solstice sunrise, the winter solstice sunrise, the spring and fall equinox sunrise and eclipse of the sun and moon. There are other more exotic alignments one of which is the major standstill northern moonrise. This occurs every six lunar cycles or every 112 years. Since the average life span of the Stonehenge person was only 30 years, the tracking of this moon position had to be transmitted orally from one generation to the next. This is an example of the keen observation, knowledge and dedication of these remarkable people.

In the 1960s it was determined by computer studies that the stone astronomical alignments placed in the ground thousands of years earlier were indeed accurate. It is astounding how primitive people with no scientific instruments could place stones in the ground in such near perfect alignments. Precious few undertakings by primitive peoples have lasted for thousands of years and even fewer undertakings have proven reliable under the exact scrutiny of modern technology. (12)

While a strong argument could be made for Stonehenge as an astronomical shrine, an equally strong argument could be made for Stonehenge as a shrine to the dead. This great gravestone is close to over three hundred prehistoric burial sites of all sizes and shapes. For many thousands of years, the powerful priests and chieftains had been buried within a "few day's walk" of Stonehenge. There are some 35 earthen causeways (parallel earth embankments) in southern England today dating back to this period and before, and some of these are miles long. There are huge earth, stone and wooden circle monuments in close proximity to Stonehenge. Many are much bigger and older and could have been used in burial rites.

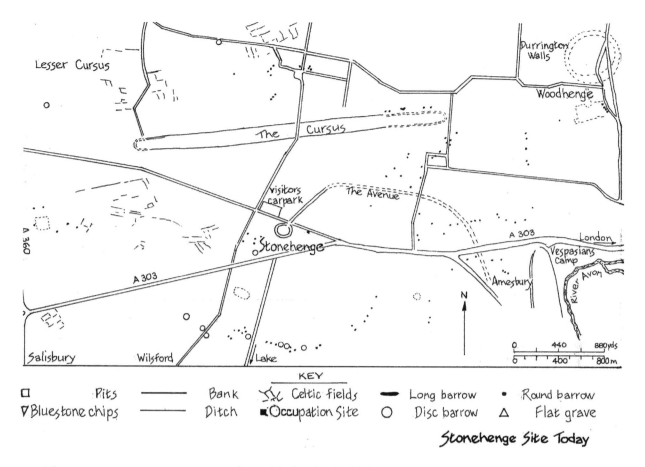

KEY

□	Pits	——	Bank	☓ Celtic fields	➤ Long barrow	• Round barrow
▽ Bluestone chips		——	Ditch	■ Occupation Site	○ Disc barrow	△ Flat grave

Stonehenge Site Today

There was an apparent preoccupation with the dead which was as strong as the preoccupation with the positions of the sun and moon. Was Stonehenge used for an astronomical monument, a shrine to the dead, a combination of both, or something else? (17)

I have great respect for the Stonehenge people. We can only conclude that they were well organized, disciplined, dedicated, peace loving and advanced in every way except literacy. They were intelligent construction engineers, superior astronomers and exceptional stone masons. They must have been very efficient farmers to support the non-farm labor force required to build Stonehenge. There were, perhaps, 120 generations of Stonehenge people, yet we know little about them as individuals because they are only identified by the great monuments they built. They were a nameless and faceless people who deserve to be remembered. We will never find a Rosetta stone revealing the mysteries of the Stonehenge people because there is no discernible written language. It is up to writers to reconstruct the past of Stonehenge, breathe life into their souls and to create saints and sinners in their novels.

The archaeological digs in close proximity to Stonehenge provide only sketchy information about these people. The first people who built Stonehenge were probably crude farmers who came to England from Europe. There is no evidence that these people were much different from modern man. Their height and weight, the color of their skin, hair and eyes could be easily matched in Britain or Ireland today. They were perhaps more wily, sinewy and more toughened by the elements than modern man. They were called "beaker people" because of ornate beakers or clay vases found in their graves. They introduced copper tools and wool clothing, and they built the original Stonehenge with the simplest bone, copper and wooden tools. (18)

Since little is known about Stonehenge people, let us look to other sources where well preserved clothing and ornaments have been found. A grave dating to a period concurrent with Stonehenge was found in Egtved, Denmark. This grave contained three corpses fully dressed and miraculously preserved from the ravages of time. It is the best information that is available, and I use this source to dress the characters in my novel. Some people have the misconception that all the Stonehenge people were barbarous spear-throwing savages who scampered about in animal skins. From what we have learned, this is not completely true. For example, the presence of flowers and embroidered neck pieces at the Egtved, Denmark, site suggests, knowledge and appreciation of the beauty of flowers and embroidered neck ware by the prehistoric persona. (19)

Female Summer Attire

Rodney Castleden has this to say about the ladies. "The ladies' hairstyles were as redundantly complex and varied as they are today. One style involved piling the hair up on the front of the head, increasing the height with a coif of false hair; the whole construction was held in place by a lozenge-meshed net made of black horse-hair and bound with interlacing cords. The horn combs women always carried with them, attached to their belts, shows that they were fastidiously concerned about their appearance. Some women wore bonnets; these were elaborately made and obviously designed to draw attention." (There was an amazing consciousness of style and appearance that we normally do not associate with prehistoric people.)

Rodney Castleden has this to say about the men. "The men's basic garment was a deceptively simple tunic that wrapped around the body from the shoulder level down to knee or mid-calf. He fastened it around his waist with a leather belt and with a leather strap over each shoulder. The cut of the breast-line varied; it could be horizontal, or sloping down to one side, or tongued up to the throat. Over this tunic he wore a knee-length woolen cape that could be round, oval or kidney-shaped; it was fastened across his chest, and the edge was flipped back at the neck and chest to form a collar and reveres. The very striking effect of the tunic and cape was enhanced by a jaunty round woolen cap, which could be either beehive or fez-shaped. The caps were made with unusual care, with several layers of cloth to make them thick and cushioned, guaranteed to keep their shape. The emphasis on bonnets and caps shows that they were the focus of attention. The cut of one's hat obviously said much about one's social status or self opinion. The men were clean-shaven and wore their hair long, combed back and parted in the middle; they also carried a comb." (20)

STONEHENGE at 1000 B.C.   My novel takes place at a time when Stonehenge was at its zenith, after 1550 B.C. Every significant stone was precisely placed, the monument was magnificent, and archaeological digs reveal that the people were prosperous. By the time Roman troops came to England in early AD, Stonehenge had been abandoned and stood in ruins. What had happened to 3,000 years or more of sun and moon worship and reverence of the dead? Why were the graves abandoned? What had happened to the attraction of the monuments and the very advanced people who populated the area? This book takes place at the end of the Stonehenge period. While my book is a novel, I have recreated this final period based on reliable facts and creditable theories that are available from archaeological and modern studies.

Some experts believe that the Stonehenge civilization might have disintegrated in just three generations, perhaps from contagious diseases and/or famine. (21) Diseases of epidemic proportion could, and did, wipe out entire communities in a short period of time. In the 1300's the Black Plague and Bubonic Plague killed a fourth of the population of Europe. As late as World War I a diphtheria and flu epidemic caused more deaths than were recorded by the conflict of the war. To a society of people not familiar with modern medicine, an epidemic could be devastating.

There were more long range factors that could effect the termination of the Stonehenge people. Stonehenge spans a time period from the neolithic age (advanced stone age) through the copper age to the bronze age. The social, economic and psychological forces brought on by the changes inherent in these time periods undoubtedly brought pressure to the way of life of the Stonehenge people. The final age, the bronze age, produced glittering gold-like tools, weapons and treasures. It emphasized wealth and power which created a society that is easier for 20th century man to recognize. There was a clear social division in labor, legal and administrative powers. It created warrior-hero cults whose exploits were written down and remembered in songs and fables. In the neolithic times there were few warrior-heroes nor was there any literature in which individual self-glorification would have been possible.

Another important factor was the wetter climate which caused over use of the farm land, economical disaster and religious disorientation. During the latter part of the Bronze Age the weather gradually became rainy, cloudy and foggy. A religious faith which relied on making celestial sightings on a regular and predictable basis would have become disoriented over time.

Climate changes caused much of the farmland to be used to exhaustion and abandoned. Much of the poor land reverted back to scrub and forest. The weather change caused great hardship to the farmers as agricultural production became less dependable and less predictable. Water-logged areas, flooding and peat bogs became more common. It is possible that the Stonehenge people in this later time period did not enjoy excess farm production and could not give time, food and labor to the priests at Stonehenge. This might have led to widespread social upheaval, population migration and abandonment of Stonehenge. (22)

Lastly it is believed that the priestly class could have misused their considerable power and knowledge. It is believed that the priest kept the succession of their knowledge within a close-knit family of priests. For example, the ability to predict the disappearance of the sun or moon (eclipse) would provide a mad priest with frightening powers over the simple farmers. (23)

"BETRAYAL AT STONEHENGE 1000 B.C." is a novel which breathes life into the souls of those extraordinary people who populated Stonehenge. This book creates saints and sinners out of the nameless and faceless people who are only identified by the great monuments they built. The setting is Stonehenge with cleverly crafted episodes about the building of Stonehenge, eclipses, ancient burial rites and bronze age life. Add to that a dash of love, lust, paranoia and murder and you have a story that is enjoyment for every Stonehenge buff, mystery novel enthusiast and science fiction reader.

REFERENCES

1. Atkinson, R.J.C. (1990), Stonehenge, Penguin PP 169
2. Chippindale, Christopher (1987), Stonehenge Complete, Cornell University Press, Chapters 1 through 6. This is an excellent story of the many colorful people who have tried to decipher Stonehenge
3. Castleden, Rodney (1990), The Stonehenge People; an exploration of the life in neolithic Britain 4700-2000B.C. PP 101. and PP 131
4. Hutton, Ronald (1995), Stonehenge and Salisbury Plain (Tape), University of Bristol, England.
5. Atkinson, R.J.C. (1990), Stonehenge, Penguin PP 25.
6. Castleden, Rodney (1990), The Stonehenge People; an exploration of the life in neolithic Britain 4700-2000B.C. PP57.
7. Renfrew, Colin (1973), Before Civilization, Alfred A. Knopf, PPS 237-239
8. Castleden, Rodney (1990), The Stonehenge people; an exploration of life in neolithic Britain 700-2000B.C. PPS 93-100, 144-145, 243-246.
9. Atkinson, R.J.C. (1990), Stonehenge, Penquin PP 24.
10. Hutton, Ronald Dr. (1995), Stonehenge and the Salisbury Plain (Tape), University of Bristol, England.
11. Chippindale, Christopher (1987), Stonehenge Complete, Cornell University Press, Chapter 4.
12. Hawkins, Gerald S. (1966), Stonehenge Decoded, Souvenir Press
13. Burgess, Colin (1980), The Age of Stonehenge, J.M Dent & Sons Ltd, PPS 117, 330-334.
14. Renfrew. Colin (1973), Before Civilization, Alfred A. Knopf, Chapter 11, PPS 214-247.
15. Renfrew, Colin (1973), Before Civilization, Alfred A. Knopf, PPS 214-217, 129.
16. Atkinson R.J.C. (1990), Stonehenge, Penguin, PPS 39-54, 56, 127, 134, 140.
17. Chippindale, Christopher (1987), Stonehenge Complete, Cornell University Press,
18. Chippindale, Christopher (1987), Stonehenge Complete, Cornell University Press, PPS 211-212. Chippindale has a more detailed study in "The Beaker Folk".
19. Castleden, Rodney (1993), The Stonehenge People; an exploration of the life in neolithic Britain 4700-2000B.C.. PPS 199-222
20. Burgess, Colin (1980), The Age of Stonehenge, J.M.Dent & Sons Ltd, PPS 180-192.
21. Hutton, Ronald (1995), Stonehenge and the Salisbury Plain (tape), University of Bristol, England.
22. Burgess, Colin (1980), The Age of Stonehenge, J.M. Dent & Sons Ltd, PPS 43, 130, 156, 237-239, 250, 257, 287, 350.
23. Atkinson, R.J.C. (1990), Stonehenge, Penguin Press. PP 172.

ILLUSTRATIONS

1. Time Chart
2. Stonehenge at the Period of the Aubrey Stones
3. Stonehenge at the Period of the Blue Stones
4. A Drawing of the Astronomical Alignments at Stonehenge
5. Map of Possible Routes Taken to Bring the Blue Stones to Stonehenge
6. Map from Marlborough Downs to Stonehenge
7. Sarsen Uprights with Mortise and Tenon Fittings and Tongue and Groove Joints
8. Erecting the Uprights
9. Stonehenge at the Period of Sarsen Stone Construction
10. Stonehenge 1000 B.C.
11. Burial Sites Today
12. Artist's Conception of Female Dress from a Danish Tree-Trunk Coffin

Contents

CHAPTER 1 CELEBRATION OF THE SUMMER SOLSTICE

The celebration of the summer solstice is the greatest holiday of the year for the people of Stonehenge. On the day of the solstice, the sun shines on the earth the longest, and it is the sun that is the center of the pilgrim's lives... the source of all creation. The sun causes every plant to start, to grow and to flourish. Barley and wheat, corn, herbs, nuts, berries-- everything must have sunlight. Even plants in the streams and ocean must have sunlight to grow. Cattle and deer grow larger and stronger when the sun shines, and the sheep grow better wool if there is abundant grass to eat. Even the wolf that lives by killing rabbits benefits when there is more plant life for the rabbit to eat. If the plants are more plentiful, then the people of Stonehenge are healthier and happier. ALL LIFE comes from the sun; take this away and the people of Stonehenge would soon die.

The Stonehenge pilgrims were gathering together in the middle of the meadow-like field within eyesight of the great Stonehenge shrine. It was important that they see the heel stone at the edge of the Stonehenge circle, because the sun would rise like a ball of fire and balance on the tip top of this stone indicating the beginning of the solstice. The clan families with the highest social rank and wealth placed their tent for the best view of the heel stone, but not too close to offend the priests. Pro's tent was at the very front of the field with a unobstructed view.

The men wore special Sunday-best linen tunics that wrapped round their bodies and hung loosely from the shoulders. The tunics was fastened around the waist with a leather belt tied together in the middle with the lacing falling down the front. Over the tunic the men wore knee-length woolen capes that were either oval or kidney shaped. It was fastened across the chest with a leather string which was decorated with semiprecious stones and good luck charms. All the clothing had been scrubbed clean, bleached in the sun and set aside for this special pilgrimage. It was the men's hats that revealed their social status and trade. The hats were woolen, with several layers of cloth to look thick and cushioned. They were shaped like a beehive, square, round and or even fez-shaped. The sheep farmer's hat had a patch of white wool fuzz sewed conspicuously on the front, while the wheat farmer had sHocks of wheat stuck in his hat. Pro had a beehive shaped hat with a large amber stone pendant sewed prominently in front. All the men were clean shaven, while the hair on their heads was long and parted in the middle.

"Jep," Pro said to his manservant, "keep a bright bonfire blazing all the time. We want all our friends and relatives to know we are here so they can join us in mead and roast mutton."

"I'll put some of these dry pine limbs on the fire." Jep pointed to a pile of brush and smiled with a toothless grin. "They will flame up and make a bright fire."

"Pro? Have you seen Zeff yet?" Qua, Pro's wife, called from inside the tent. Pro heard but he did not answer. "Pro?" Pro stepped inside the tent and looked at Qua combing her black hair with a comb carved out of a sheep's horn. Her hair was piled up on the front of her head, increasing her height with a coil of false hair. She was placing a lozenge-meshed net made of horse hair on her head.

"No," Pro sighed. He dropped down on the pile of skins beside her. He knew she was hoping that he and Zeff could be friends and family again.

"Isn't it dangerous for us to be here when you and Zeff are so mad at each other?" She stopped her combing, turned and looked directly at Pro.

"I'm not mad at him - I've never been mad at him. It's just that he is so -- so touched by the moon's powers," Pro snapped back. It's like I said, I think he's lost his mind to the dark side of the moon. He has got to tell the people what is going to happen. He has got to. -- He must!"

"But if he doesn't, won't it be dangerous for us here? Who knows what he will do to you and me -- and to the children?" She stopped combing her hair and looked directly at Pro. "Pro, you have to do something!"

"It is not for me to go to the chief priest of Stonehenge and request a visit. If he wants to see me, he can have one of his attendant priests come and get me."

Qua feverishly started combing her hair, her forehead furrowed and her face severe. She put the comb down with a thump. "Pro, I'm so worried."

Pro moved over to her and touched her shoulder. "I'm worried too," he whispered in her ear, gently rubbing the strained muscles in her neck and back. "But we can't let this ruin our stay at Stonehenge this summer solstice. Can we? We have too many relatives to see and visit. Besides, I don't think Zeff will do anything to us. It isn't like him. I mean, he is my cousin. I know him."

"You're right," she said after a pause. She stood up and they hugged each other closely. Pro continued to rub her neck and back, his way of saying he understood her fears. She put her head on his shoulder and looked up into his eyes and they hugged again. The fears that they shared seemed to melt away for the moment.

The pungent smell of onions and garlic mixed with the smell of freshly cooked mutton filled the air. Spits were in place, with venison roasting over fires of alder and oak. Children were sitting around the fire playing with little sticks and stones of all shapes. Embellished by a fertile childhood imagination, the sticks and stones became mothers, fathers, hunters, and all sorts of attacking wild beasts.

Pro was bent over a spit, allowing the juice from a succulent piece of mutton to fall to the ground when Kim called, "Pro, come over to our fire. I haven't seen you for awhile." Kim was a trader in slaves that Pro used to deal with. He smiled broadly, tipped his square shaped hat and motioned for Pro to join him. "Take a look at these," Kim said as he held open the flap of his tent. Lounging on woolen blankets were seven young girls from fifteen to eighteen years old. Their curved bodies were briefly attired in the finest of deer skin clothing. They were busy sewing small pieces of leather together into a cape. "Which one do you want?" Kim said with a devilish smile.

"Which one? Ha! That's impossible to say." Pro held his hand up in a hopeless gesture. "I like them all." Pro was trying to be diplomatic since all the girls were hanging on his every word. They all wanted to be the property of a wealthy trading family. Pro really didn't want a slave girl now because he was comfortable with his wife. Qua had become more than a chattel. She was a trusting wife and a loving mother to their children. Pro knew she would not say anything if he bought a pretty slave girl, and he was certainly tempted. But she would not be pleased either, and it would be a source of trouble in the future. Something had happened between Qua and himself. Pro had grown to respect and love her, and she had become part of him. He had no desire to disrupt that.

"They are all really beautiful," Pro admitted. He walked into the tent and smiled at the first girl he met, and she smiled back. All the girls had straight blond hair which draped down to their shoulders and then fell to their midriffs. They were not slave girls from neighboring clans, for their eyes were blue and their skin was fair. Slave girls from neighboring clans had black hair, a tanned complexion and round, oval faces. The blond slaves were unique to the Stonehenge people and a status symbol for the owner. Pro knew that they came the Baltic sea region by the northern merchants who traded at the northern channel coast.

One motioned Pro over to her side. When he least expected it she jumped up, threw her body at him and hugged him tightly. "Take me out of here," she begged. Pro was pleasantly befuddled, and he didn't know if she was earnestly pleading or just being playful. While he rather enjoyed her attention, he slowly disengaged her and backed off with an approving smile.

"How much for all seven of them?" he teased.

"Oh ho! You want all seven, do you?" Kim laughed. "Seven young girls like these would put you in an early grave." They both laughed. "Besides, I can't trade all seven."

"No? Why not? I'm sure you brought them all to the solstice to trade." Pro was curious.

"Zeff wants six of them for himself and the other priests."

"Oh, is that right? I've heard that Zeff has had a lot of slave girls lately."

Kim nodded as he looked over his shoulder to make sure no one was within earshot, then whispered, "And they all end up as sacrifices to the gods." They exchanged incredulous glances.

Pro put his hand to his mouth and whispered, "That's hard to believe, Kim. That's more sacrifices than I can remember from any priest -- or any Stonehenge chieftain for that matter." Slaves were property, and an owner could do with them as he pleased. Occasionally, when times were very bad, a slave owner would offer his slave for sacrifice. It had happened, but what Zeff was doing was murderously unacceptable, and both of them knew it.

"I don't know what to say," said Kim. "If Zeff wants six beautiful maidens, Zeff gets six beautiful maidens. It's too dangerous to try to interfere." Kim leaned even closer, cupped his hands over his mouth and whispered. "And some say that Zeff can't father any children -- can't raise it up -- that he becomes violent and blames it on the maidens, then sacrifices them to the gods."

"Oh, I didn't know that," Pro said tersely. They both decided it was best to dismiss the subject, they saluted each other, and went on their way.

Pro wandered through the crowd greeting friends at every turn. He had traded with most of them and knew many of them by name. He greeted Abt, a farmer friend who grew emmer wheat and naked barley. Abt tipped his oval shaped hat, which had sprigs of wheat shocks sticking out of it. "I could sure use some of those precious stones you get," he said coming quickly to the point and chewing on each word.

"Precious stones? I don't know exactly what you mean. Do you mean those beautiful beads that I get from sea merchants I meet at the north coast?" Pro questioned. "They come from far away, from a place called Egypt, and they are very expensive."

Farmer Abt shook his head and squinted his eyes as if he had tasted something bitter. "No, no, those beads are those little stones that shine in the sunlight, aren't they? Stuff that women wear. No, that's not it." Pro nodded. "I want that tan colored stuff that shines."

"Oh, you mean amber? I get that from the sea merchants up north too. That comes from traders far away on the Baltic Sea. And that is very expensive too. Only the chieftains and the priests can afford amber rings and pendants."

"Rings and pendants? No - o." Abt took off his hat and scratched the snarled hair on his head. "That's not it either. It's more yellow in color and sparkles in the sunlight."

" You're not thinking about gold, are you?" He could not begin to afford something made of gold, Pro thought.

"Noo, I know what gold is. It isn't gold, but it sometimes is the same color as gold."

"I know what you want, Abt. It's bronze -- bronze tools and knives."

"That's what I want. Something with a hard, sharp edge that cuts hay easily."

"I have all kinds of bronze tools for the farm. Tools to cut the wheat and slaughter the cattle. I will remember you the next time I have bronze ware and I'll bring it to your farm."

"Yes, I'll need some good tools, yes, the emmer crop should be good this year." He nodded his head. "I only have tools made of flint, like this." He held up his spear with a flint stone head that was shaped like an elongated heart but severely chipped and dull from years of use.

Pro held the spear in his hand. It was old and out of balance, and the flint point was loosely tied down. Three cross marks were carved on the wooden rod. "You got three deer, eh?" Pro asked.

"Two red deer and a shed deer," said Abt with a proud toothless grin. "I know that it's old and the point is wobbly, but I know how to hurl it right on the target."

"I'll get you a new spear with a bronze head, too." Precious stones, Pro thought. How could he ever think that bronze was a precious stone?

"The sun god has been kind to us since the spring time of equal days and nights, and my crops have a good start."

"Yes, it has been a warm spring," Pro agreed.

"We need the Sun God to help us in the summer, too. To give us a sign at this summer solstice that we will have enough rain and warm weather the rest of the summer for a good crop this fall."

"The weather is fair tonight. If this weather holds up we should have a definite sign from the Sun God of three, maybe four more full moons of favorable weather."

"I hope so," Abt said. Good luck." They parted, and Pro was on his way.

There appeared a man who had a pet brown bear. He called it his pet, but he had a firm leather muzzle over its mouth, and he led the animal with a strong leash. The tips of its claws had been cut down to rounded edges, but the bear was hardly tame. It never ceased looking for opportunities to escape. The bear was well trained and the man had the bear jump through a hoop, lie on his back and stand on its hind legs while the children laughed and giggled at every antic. They were full of prolonged "ohs" and "ahs" and jumped up and down in place making them as much entertainment as the bear.

Friends gathered together to sing old familiar chants and songs that had been handed down from their parents and grandparents. Some held hands and joined in a great circle, weaving back and forth in rhythm with the music. Some danced in long parallel lines where they met in the middle, slapped their hands together and shouted a greeting in unison. Others stood along the side-lines and played instruments made from hollow reeds and drums. Still others simply danced in place, inspired by the repetitive rhythmic chants.

A perfect day had passed into a perfect night. The sky was clear, and a full moon bathed the landscape with silver gray light. A slight balmy night breeze felt cool and refreshing after the hot day. Music and merriment filled the air, and the evening gradually slipped by and became morning. They had celebrated all day and all night and eagerly greeted the summer solstice sun rising over the heel stone.

Finally a priest appeared and spoke;

The sun peeks over the hill announcing dawn at summer solstice.
Its golden orange halo fused day's light with night's mist.
The full sun's light crowned the ancient heel stone.
Blinding brilliant beams of radiant white light fan in all directions.
Fleeting rainbows sparkle in diamond water drops around the perimeter.
Mortals cannot look directly in the light.
Nor should they.
The sun is too powerful to see, as the sun is too omnipotent to understand.
Its warmth wed with watered earth sprouts stone-like seeds into plants.
All plants and all mankind flourish in great abundance.
Summer solstice sun shines supreme the day it smiles on earth the longest.

Man worships his heavenly benefactor and stands in exaltation where pristine beauty and benefactor are wed as One.

CHAPTER 2   THE SINISTER DARKNESS

The beginning of a perfect summer day and a promising future was abruptly changed by a strange darkening in the sky. The morning light was fading and the day was becoming gloomy, as if storm clouds had gathered, but there were no clouds in sight. The sky became dull and gray where the worshipers were camped. Strangely, the sun was still shining in full brightness a hundred paces off to the left.

At first, the dullness was slight and no one noticed. They were busy preparing morning food for the last meal they would have together before they would part. Kim, the slave trader, noticed the dullness but simply shrugged his shoulders and gave the whole incident scant attention. He was more interested in the aroma of fried pigeon eggs cooking on a wood fire.

Jep was carefully reducing the fire from flames to bright cherry red coals for cooking. He was totally preoccupied with preparing a palatable breakfast of leftover mutton, wheat mush and,--Pro's favorite -- a hot drink prepared from crushed, roasted dandelion roots.

Slowly, but inexorably, more and more of the sun was disappearing from sight. The day became darker and cooler only where Pro's party was camped. Off to the right or left there was still daylight. A wall of blackness was approaching. It looked as if a huge black storm cloud were moving over the sun.

Finally, a curious and disturbed group of the faithful simply stopped all activity and stood in awe and dismay. The bear trainer stared at the sky with his mouth hung open. "It's not a cloud, is it?" he said softly to no one in particular. He rubbed his eyes and looked at the sky again. "It's not blurred eyes, and I'm not moon struck." He shook his head in disbelief. "I've never seen anything like this before. Have you?"

"No, I haven't" Pro said. He stood still with his hands on his hips and looked up at the strange occurrence. "It's, it's frightening." Everyone was becoming alarmed.

"Great God of the Sun, what is it?" the bear trainer blurted out loud enough for everyone to hear. "You!" He turned to Pro. "You, you've turned silver. Your face, your hat all have a silver tint. Even your hair on your arms looks like fine strands of silver. The grass is gray and silver. Great God of the Sun, what is it!?"

Pro looked at the bear trainer's bear and its black fur was tinctured with a fringe of silver. A haunting feeling crept over Pro, for now this wild animal looked like a beast from the underworld. The beast nervously paced back and forth, its tongue dangling from its mouth with silver tinted droplets of saliva dripping to the ground. Pro shivered, for the sight scared him and he quickly looked away.

A huge black disk was devouring the sun. As it moved to cover the sun it sucked light from the earth. There was no stopping it.

Qua came out of the tent. "Look how dark it has become! I - I can hardly see you. What's wrong?" She put her hand over her mouth. "Oh God of fertility, have my eyes failed me? Am I going blind? What's wrong?" She rubbed her eyes.

"Qua, nothing is wrong with you. It's- it's just that the sun is disappearing." Pro swallowed hard and could barely get the words out of his mouth. Qua rushed to his side and Pro hugged her warm body as tightly as he could. Pro's dog, who always greeted them with enthusiasm, had crawled under a woolen blanket where he was whimpering. The birds had abandoned the blacked out area and were flying to light.

"Jep, make as big a bonfire as you can. We must be able to see, and keep warm too." Then Pro pointed. "Look over there! You can see the stars in the sky as if it were night. There's the big northern star." All eyes gazed at the star, but no one knew what to say.

A strange chirping sound commenced and everyone looked at each other in wonderment. First the sound came from the tent, then under the wood pile and finally from all directions. "It's crickets chirping," shouted Kim. "The crickets are chirping just like night." The crowd simply stood silent, frozen in total bewilderment.

The sun was now more than half covered. The sinister blackness continued creeping over the sky.

Fear penetrated the souls of the people assembled and the first cries were weak and pleading. "Help, oh help us get back the sun." This was followed by a crescendo of cries and pleas. Some began beating sticks against anything that would make a sound. Heart rending bedlam came from every quarter.

It looked like the center of the sun had been punched out. Around the disk there was a blazing brilliant halo of light, as if the sun were trying desperately to shine but could not. The sun, the very source of all life and fertility, was being swallowed up by a supernatural force, turning black and cold. A relentless, unexplained force, which was sinister and foreboding, had taken hold.

Many worshipers simply stood still, fixed in place, staring at the darken sun. They reached out to find someone's hand to hold. The warmth of a live human being in a world which had become dead and cold was the only assurance they had. Some became sick and vomited on the ground.

The great monument of Stonehenge had now completely disappeared in darkness. The giant sarsen stone circle was lost and the five massive trilithon arches of the horseshoe, the very symbol of strength and stability, had silently vanished. The beautiful blue stone circle -- gone. The heel stone, the slaughter stone, the four station stones, even the circle earth embankment and the ditch were consumed by darkness. At first the worshipers did not notice that Stonehenge had vanished from sight. Then came the most pitiful, agonizing cry. "Where is Stonehenge? All is lost! All is lost!" The holy link between the Stonehenge people on earth and their gods in the heaven had been severed. They felt adrift in the sea of blackness.

Zeff, the high priest, finally appeared and climbed up on the heel stone. He seemed weak and frail and he had to be held on top of the pyramid, capped stone. The commotion stopped as a frightened group gathered around to hear. "The sun has disappeared," he said to a blackened faceless audience. "The Sun God is very angry with us. He is angry because one of us has failed him."

There was booing and grumbling in the crowd. "Why is he angry? What can we do?" The crowd was frantic, and their questions were converging out of the darkness on the chief priest.

"What must we do?"

"Stonehenge is gone. Gone."

"Will we ever see summer again?"

"My crops will die without the sun!"

Zeff finally waved his hand to stop the questions, but no one could see him. Then he shouted, "The sun is gone and will return only if you obey me."

"We'll obey you. Tell us what to do!"

"Yes, What can we do?"

"Who did this?"

Zeff looked as if he would faint. In a weak voice barely audible he said, "It is Pro the trader, son of Gor of the Nese clan. He did this. He did not obey." Zeff coughed, cleared his throat and continued, "He would not obey me and the Gods are angry. Now we all must suffer." Zeff seemed to bring forth some reserve strength. He pulled himself higher on the heel stone and peered into the blanket of darkness. "Pro is out there somewhere. Find Pro."

"Pro, where are you? We want Pro. We want Pro!" The chant became louder and more pronounced. "We want Pro."

"What did he do?" one asked.

Someone from the corner of the crowd called in a booming voice, "Pro caused the sun to disappear. Kill Pro, kill him." Others joined in "Kill him! Kill him! Where is Pro?!"

6

CHAPTER 3 ZEFF'S MISSION FIVE YEARS EARLIER

Zeff and Pro were cousins, nearly the same age, and from the beginning they were very close. Even as a child, Zeff wanted to be chief priest at Stonehenge. His father was chief priest, and his grandfather was chief priest before him. Priesthood was in his blood almost as if it had been an inherited right. When Pro and Zeff were children, Zeff would play-act that he was a priest. He liked to entertain his young friends by telling them that the moon would rise at a certain place in the sky. At high noon he would pound two stakes in the ground, and when it became dark the stakes would be lined in the direction of the moonrise. Or he would tell stories of ghostly spirits that walked through the stone arches at Stonehenge after dark and his young friends would believe him.

The young men who were going to be priests did not have to work in the fields but were given special training by the senior priests. Zeff learned how to predict the exact location of the sunrise and sunset in the sky, and to tell when and where the moon would rise and set at exact times of the year. He learned the many fertility rites, burial rites, dances and songs. The training was an intense and exclusive secret study for the priests only. Zeff would show Pro some of the rites when his father was not around -- like the sleight of hand trick where a rabbit's foot disappears in the air. In another rite, Zeff would make a goat disappear in a cloud of reddish brown dust of ocher powder. Zeff's young friends were always amazed and a bit frightened that a trusted priest knew such deception.

It was five summer solstices ago, soon after the winter solstice, when Zeff became chief priest at Stonehenge. He invited Pro, his mate Qua, and their twin children Ola and Oma, to visit with him. "This is indeed an honor to see Stonehenge firsthand, Zeff," Pro said. "We have never stood within the great circle of arches and seen the altar stone. Standing here by the altar stone is reserved for the high priests only, isn't it?"

"Well, as chief priest, I decide who can come inside the great circle," Zeff said with a confident smile. He wore a pure white robe made of a rare albino deer fur which flared out from the shoulders and extended to his ankles. It showed no shape of his body, looking like a handbell turned upside down. "I know you, above all, would appreciate the secrets of this place." He continued, "So many of the farmers just don't know anything about the alignments of stones. They don't care either. It's a shame." He pointed to the huge arched stones arranged as a horseshoe around the altar stone, and the massive stone circle about eighteen feet high capped with perfectly level stone tops. "The open end of the horseshoe faces the heel stone over there just outside the earth ditch." Zeff pointed.

"Look, Father, those stone pillars are so-oo big," said Ola, age nine. He threw his head back and looked towards the top of the 25 - foot pillar.

Zeff smiled, pleased that Ola showed so much interest. "They are big, maybe several times as big as you, Ola and Oma, and grand old stones too." Zeff glanced up at the massive arches and with satisfaction. "And they are aligned to tell us a lot about the sun and moon." Zeff moved the party along to a special spot in the very heart of the circle behind the altar stone. Sighting a line from where he was standing through the arches to a pillar on the outer circle, he stuck his cane in the ground and said, "That's the eastern point." Then he made the same sighting in a westerly direction, took a step to the left and then a half step back. "That's the spot. Yes, indeed. That's the exact spot." He moved his cane to the new spot and stuck it in the soft ground. "Stand here behind my cane, Ola. and Oma. I want to show you something you will never forget."

The twins looked towards their mother and smiled. Qua smiled back encouraging them to join Zeff. Zeff stooped to the twins' level and put his arm on their shoulders, his eyes twinkling for he was delighted with their interest. "There is the heel stone," he whispered as if it were their secret. "The sun rises over the heel stone every summer solstice signaling the longest daylight of the year. Do you know what the summer solstice is?"

"Oh, yes. The summer solstice is the time of year that we come to Stonehenge to play games, said Ola.

"And have picnics," added Oma. "Don't forget the picnics with all our friends."

Zeff glanced up at Pro under a raised eyebrow. "The midsummer sunrise is much more than that. It marks the furthest point north that the sun will ever rise in a year, and it is also the longest day of the year."

"I like the summer solstice time," said Ola.

"In the spring, at the time of equal days and nights, the sun rises over there in the east." Zeff pointed with his cane and aligned his vision between several stone monuments. "As the year advances, the sunrise moves northwards towards the summer solstice sunrise. Then the sun stops moving northward and moves back southeast again until it rises over here due west." He pointed again to the line of direction of several stone markers. "This is the autumn time of equal days and nights. In the winter half of the year, the sunrise advances southwards until it rises over there." He pointed. "That is called the winter solstice."

"Wow, I didn't know that the sun moved around the sky that much," said Ola.

"Of course it does," Oma corrected her brother, "you just haven't noticed it."

Zeff rose to his full stature smiling approvingly at the young twins. He turned to Pro and said, "Pro, I want your opinion on something that I think would interest you. Come." Pro was flattered that Zeff would seek out his opinion. From childhood Pro and Zeff had talked over everything, even the most technical theological questions. Other children would laugh at Zeff and even avoid him, but Pro did not. Now that Zeff was chief priest, he sought Pro's opinion and he was pleased and eager to help.

Zeff wanted Pro's opinion but it was on a subject completely different than Pro expected. "Pro, we need to train young people to continue the line of succession of priests at Stonehenge. I think that Ola would be a good priest. I know he is too young now, but someday, before you know it, he will be ready." Zeff smiled broadly. "I would be honored to teach him."

Pro looked back and forth between Qua and the twins. "Well, we certainly are honored, Zeff. We shall look forword to the day when they are old enough to leave their parents and train with you. But there are two of them, you know. They are twins, and they are almost inseparable. They play together and work together all the time." Pro shrugged his shoulders.

"We can talk about that later," Zeff said. He waved his hand in the air and Yam, one of his assistant priests, appeared. "Join us with some mead and apples at the shelter." Pro and his family were led inside a small shelter a hundred paces away from Stonehenge. Zeff pulled back a tarpaulin under which there were two moist clay tablets about a yard square which had been rolled smooth and were the consistency of bread dough. Sketched on one tablet was a schematic drawing of 22 different sight lines of the sun and moon rising and setting throughout the year. On the other tablet was mounted a miniature model of Stonehenge with all the stones and pillars made to scale.

"Zeff, this is wonderful - you being chief priest and all. Just what you always wanted." Pro studied the sketches in silence for what seemed like hours, he was totally absorbed with the enormity of the structure.

Zeff took Ola and Oma by their arms and pointed to a spot on the clay map. "This marks the most northerly position of the midwinter moonrise through six lunar cycles. Do you know what that means?"

They nodded "No" and looked up to Zeff with innocent smiles.

The twins looked at their mother for further counsel but she smiled and said "I don't know either."

Zeff laughed, "Well, let me tell you then. The moon rises at that point once every 112 summer solstices, and it is a great feast day."

"Wow!" said Ola. "That's ancient."

"That's older than grand dad," continued Oma.

"Shh," said Qua. "Your grand dad wouldn't like that."

"How do you know that, Zeff?" questioned Pro. He put his hands on his hips. "Just how do you keep track of the time? Let's see, you are 26 summer solstices old now. Your father, my uncle Lop, was 46 summer solstices old when he died. So, how do you know when 112 summer solstices have passed? Is it inscribed on this clay tablet?"

Zeff laughed. He leaned forward, bowed slightly and pointed to his head. "It's all up here. You see, my father gave me the information, and I will pass it on to the next high priest. This is what we learned when we were training to become priests when we were Ola's age." He smiled confidently. "And we will never miss this moonrise feast. Never!"

8

Pro sighed. "Something confuses me, Zeff."

"What is it?"

"How can Stonehenge be the place where so many sun and moon combinations can be seen?" Pro pointed to the clay tablet that showed 22 alignments of the sun and moon. "Is Stonehenge the only place for all those sightings?"

Zeff turned and looked squarely at Pro for he was dead serious. "Pro, this is holy ground." His voice dropped to a hush. "It's true. This is holy ground!"

Pro asked. "What do you mean?"

"Yes. Avebury doesn't have as many sightings, and neither does Woodhenge or any other shrine in this country. It's holy ground, blessed by the gods, and that's all there is to it. There is nothing like it." His eyes sparkled and he smiled broadly. He put his arms around Pro and Qua's shoulders. "It's a special place!" He nodded his head affirmatively. "It is the only place in all the land where the gods in heaven have allowed us to see so many sun and moon sightings."

Pro thought of the many shrines within two or three days walking distance from Stonehenge. There were thirty, maybe forty, with earthen ditches and stone circles but none were as grand as Stonehenge.

The spell was broken when Yam arrived with drinks, and Zeff proposed, "A toast to our meeting today. To you and your good mate and son. I'm so glad you came." Everyone drank a long swig of mead.

"Wow, this is good." Ola looked at the mead in his beaker and swirled it around. "Dad, what is mead?"

"Mead is honey and water mixed together. Then you must allow it to set for at least three full moons so it will have a tingle," Qua volunteered. "It's good, isn't it?"

"Zeff, here's a toast to your new position as chief priest," Pro said. "I know you have wanted this all your life, and you will be the best priest Stonehenge ever had." Broad smiles appeared on everyone's faces and they touched bowls and drank again.

"My success here is based on priests like Yam." Zeff smiled and patted Yam on the shoulder. "Yam's responsibility is to determine when the next eclipse of the sun and moon will occur, which means that he must remember so many things about the sun and the moon and keep them all straight in his head. It is very important." Yam smiled broadly. "A toast to friends and to the greatness of Stonehenge." All joined him. Yam bowed politely to everyone and left. Pro noticed a pink white scar across his left cheek which Yam frequently rubbed when he was nervous.

"Do you know what an eclipse is, Pro?" Zeff asked.

"It's when the sun moves in front of the moon and cuts off its light. Or when the moon moves in front of the sun and cuts off its light." Pro's explanation was brief but adequate.

"Pro, there is something that has been bothering me and I need your opinion." Zeff paused and stroked his pointed beard, choosing his words carefully. "Pro, as you know, at a specific time each year the summer solstice occurs. Then we wait for many sunsets and the summer solstice occurs again." He paused. Pro nodded agreement. "This means a fixed time in the year can be set by observation of summer solstice. Using that fixed time, let us count the days from summer solstice to summer solstice."

"Wait, I don't understand. Summer is summer and winter is winter -- why count the days? Besides, all the days are different. There are shorter in the winter, and colder too -- less sunshine." Pro shrugged his shoulders, "I don't understand."

"I've changed a few things at Stonehenge. Defined things differently here and there," Zeff said with a confident smile. "We measure days from sunrise to sunrise now. It doesn't matter how much sunlight there is in each day."

These words struck Pro as cold and foreign. Warm summer days were so essential to the farmers and the growing of their crops. On the cold winter days nothing grew. The fertility cycle, the core of the religion, was based the warmth and light from the sun. Pro didn't understand. He interpreted Zeff's definition as disregarding the sanctity of the sun. "Why are you doing this?" He shook his head in disbelief. "Why are you changing things so?"

"We didn't count the days before because we saw no need to. The sun god has given us great knowledge - great knowledge." Zeff paused, then said softly, "We didn't use the knowledge that the sun god has provided us, and that's wrong.

9

"Wrong? What do you mean?"

"We didn't reckon time in any meaningful way. By counting the days, we can determine time to start planting and when to harvest, when to have festivals and when to worship the gods."

"I still don't see how you could use this."

"The farmers would benefit most, at first. They can start farming early and we can have a longer growing season. Better crops!"

"What do the farmers think?"

"Well, I've already told the farmers to start planting."

"It's too soon to start planting, isn't it?" Pro thought about the blue gray and tan wheatear, the first bird to return after winter. In his mind he heard the squeaky, warbling song of the bird as it chased spring insects on the ground. They had not yet arrived, and that was the surest and earliest sign of the spring that Pro knew. "It's too soon to plant, Zeff. We may still have some frost."

"The farmers want to start as early as possible," retorted Zeff.

"This idea of yours might have some problems." Pro argued. "I would have a trial this spring and see how it would work out. I would mark numbers and days down on your clay." Pro pointed to the clay and made a small mark with his fingernail. "Something like this. - Then it depends on the weather. It may be too early to plow this year, or maybe it's all right. You don't know for sure. When you are sure, then direct the farmers."

"No one remembers how cold it was more than three seasons back. It is impossible to measure."

"And the farmers. What do they think?" Pro reminded him.

"Ah, the farmers, they always do just what they are told. They trust me. They trust me when I tell them it's time to plant. They trust me." It was clear that Zeff had made up his mind.

Pro took another sip of the mead leaving most of it in the bowl. It was oppressively sweet. Like Zeff, it came on strong and had to be taken in small portions.

CHAPTER 4 ABT THE FARMER

That spring, five summer solstices ago, Abt planted his crops early as Zeff had instructed. He feared it was too early and that there might be more cold weather. The apple trees had begun to leaf but only slightly. The blackberries and the sloe berries were showing tips of green on their branches. "If the earth goddess wanted an early spring, she would have had her plants grow sooner," he said to his wife. "They haven't grown any earlier this year."

"You know if the chief priest says that the plowing should begin earlier this year, then it will begin earlier. Zeff and all those priests at Stonehenge know what they are doing. We must trust them," said Ban, Abt's mate.

"I know, I know. But the wheat and barley need continual warm weather to start growing. You know that. And when they first start growing, they need more warm weather and a gentle rain. It has been that way since the beginning of time." He got a leather cup full of water and drank. It was very cool and refreshing. "Do you want some water?" he offered.

Ban found it difficult to get comfortable on her bed of flax and straw for she was very pregnant. "No," she said faintly as she shifted from one position to another. "Not now."

"Can I help you?" Ban looked like she was going to fall out of her bed onto the floor and Abt rushed to her, spilling some water on the hard earth floor of their hut. "Are you sure you don't want a drink?"

"I'm all right, Abt. You just continue what you are doing and I'll be all right. I'll let you know when I need help." It's an old and unfair story, thought Abt. Men have had to wait, just helplessly wait, while their mates give birth. He wanted to do something to help, but what?

"This place smells bad. It smells like wet hay." He jumped up and threw back the skin over the door. "There, now we have some fresh air." He took a deep breath of the cool air coming through the doorway. "I could get some meadowsweet and fresh hay and spread it on the floor. Meadowsweet would make it smell like roses, and we would have the best smelling hut we can for our baby."

Ban said nothing but she peered back at Abt and her eyes said, "You were never concerned about the smell before. What has gotten into you?"

"Well, I could go hunt some deer. We surely could use the meat, and if I kill a buck I could make the antler into a pick spade for the garden. There are probably some red deer over by the salt lick."

She simply shook her head. "No."

"I could fix the outside wall. The wattle needs some patching, and I could cut some twigs to weave into the wattle. I could get some mud at the stream and finish the job in no time."

"No. I could use some water now." She rolled over onto her back, and Abt noticed perspiration on her face.

He brought her a gourd of water. Then he dipped a pad of dried moss in the water and placed it on her forehead. He noticed that she was feverish and wondered if that was normal at childbirth or if Ban was sick in some way.

She drank the refreshing water, then took his rough weathered hand and held it on her belly right over the bulge from the baby. She squeezed it gently. "Do you feel our baby?" she asked.

"I do." He squeezed back, then lay down to snuggle beside her. He knew that she was already hot, so the warmth from his body would not be welcome.

The spell was broken when he rose and said, "I could go and look for a better ard plow in the forest. I know that there are some old twisted tree trunks down by the swamp that we could fashion into a really good ard."

"Oh no, no!" Ban's face was twisted, "That is too much work." Ban associated the ard with the hard work they had plowing the soil. They plowed first back and forth and the stubborn clods of dirt would not break up because they were held together by the early spring frost and wetness. They had to plow the field at right angles to the furrows to ready the soil for planting. The ard plow broke before they were done and Abt had to search through the forest and find another crooked tree trunk to fashion into an ard to finish the job. It took precious time away from the field work. Ban and Abt had worked relentlessly, every daylight hour every day to make up for the lost time. It was a killing memory. "No, please don't leave to get another ard."

She panted and perspired profusely now. "Ban, do you want me to get a midwife? Clo is just over the hill and I can be back before you know it."

She was restless, unable to get comfortable. "Oh, yes. Yes, I need her. Please go, but hurry." Her face was even more twisted and contorted than before. "I need help. GO! GO!!" Then she fell back on her pad.

Abt grabbed his walking stick and was on his way in one swift motion. He ran towards Clo's hut as fast as he could. Abt believed that Ban was not due for another full moon. He thought it took ten full moons for the gestation period, but he didn't know.

He kept running, noticing where little green blades of wheat and barley had sliced through the clods in his field. He and Ban had worked hard to get that field planted, and now it was beginning to sprout. He thought that the crops seemed to be doing well, and perhaps Zeff was right after all.

He kept running for he didn't dare to stop. He ran past the small box-like shrine which held a clay earth-goddess statue, a phallic symbol and two flint balls. When Ban first became pregnant Apt had carefully placed the skeleton of his father in front of the shrine. He believed that the earth-goddess would receive the dead spirit and put it into Ban's womb for rebirth. Abt faithfully believed that this regeneration had happened to him. He was frequently told that his fuzzy head of hair looked like his father's. He was also reminded that his short stocky frame and barrow chest were exactly like his father's. His father slipped on a slimy wet stone, fell, hit his head on a rock at the river. He drowned many summer solstices ago. Truly his father's spirit had entered his body and stayed.

The sun was setting, and he knew that he would not have much time before dark. He didn't like to be out at night because of the evil spirits that roamed in the darkness causing constant danger.

He soon saw the thatched roof of Clo's hut in the distance. "It's not far now," he thought as he ran up the hill in front of Clo's hut. It never seemed like a steep hill before, but it was steep today. He put everything he could into climbing the hill. Finally he burst into Clo's hut and shouted, "Clo, Clo, Ban is having her baby. Come quickly!" He didn't know why he expected Clo to be sitting there waiting for him but he did. The hut was empty and he looked in her farm yard, but did not find her. He looked at the raised granaries and the beehives, but Clo was not there. He called out, but she did not respond. He scanned the fields where her sheep were grazing, but she was not there either. He smelled the hay in the racks and the sheep feces on the ground and he called out again and again but no one responded. He sat on the steps of her hut pondering what to do next.

Very dark clouds had blown in dominating the sky. The air had cooled, and a cold rain commenced to fall. Abt did not notice the cold because his thoughts were only about getting Clo to help Ban. Clo finally appeared on the horizon. "Clo, Clo," he shouted. "Ban is having her baby! You've got to come!"

Clo was carrying a big wooden bowl of fresh mushrooms, but she came running when she heard Abt's call. "That's wonderful, Abt, just wonderful." She squeezed his hand and greeted him with a broad smile. "Let's go. You may need some fresh mushrooms for supper tonight." She smiled. "Now Abt, there is something I want to say. I have been midwife to many mothers and there is one thing you must do to help."

"Oh, what's that?" Abt asked.

"Stay out of the hut."

"Stay out of the hut?"

"That's right. This is a women's affair. Men just get in the way and are not allowed."

Abt nodded his head in agreement, though he didn't know why, and they ran off as fast as they could.

It was raining hard now, and the cold, wet skin clothing stuck on Clo's and Abt's backs making running difficult. The blackness of evening made footing unpredictable, and Clo had slipped several times and spilled most of the mushrooms. It was thundering constantly, and the deafening noise made them cringe in fear. Why were the rain gods angry? What were the gods trying to tell Abt and Clo? When they arrived, the hut was completely dark but Abt thought little of that. Ban barely had strength enough to drink water, let alone lay a fire. Time and time again the eerie blue-gray lighting flashed creating only a black outline of the hut.

"I'll make a fire so we can have heat and light in the hut," he said to Clo. "Then I'll leave the hut and you can call me when you need me."

"Good," said Clo. "I'll see how Ban is."

"And I'll get some dry wood." They parted.

"Oh, oooh, no!" came a shrill screech from Clo. Clo was a tough Stonehenge woman hardened by plagues, deadly disease, brutal attacks by wild animals and other hardships. She seldom showed any outward emotion but what she saw on the mud floor made her scream for help. Stretched out across the floor was Ban. The baby was half outside and half yet unborn. Clo felt them and both were cold and dead. There was a look of terror on Ban's face. Her eyes were open and her mouth twisted in pain. She had tried, but she had not been able to deliver her baby alone.

The rain and the cold continued. First it saturated the soil and plants, and then it gradually turned to ice and froze the tender young sprouts. Snow followed, blanketing the ground, and the freeze held for six days. Virtually all of the crops Stonehenge farmers had planted were destroyed that year. Abt's fields were ruined. What little grain he could save he had to use for the next year's seed, and it took him three summer solstices to accumulate enough grain to completely seed his fields again. It might have taken longer had it not been for Pro's help. He provided grain seed he got from Cornwall, and Abt didn't have to settle with Pro till he had a good crop.

While his fields produced nothing to eat, Abt found sustenance elsewhere. He was forced to gather food where he could instead of planting and raising his own. He found some grain food from patches of knotweed, chickweed, morning glory seeds and flax. From the milkweed plant he produced four dishes. The sprouts, new leaves, unopened flower buds and young pods were all satisfying when the bitterness was boiled out. From dandelion blossoms he made delicious wine for a winter drink, and from the roots he made soup, but this was not enough to sustain life.

If it had not been for a large stand of the cattails in a nearby swamp he would not have survived. In the spring, the green bloom spikes and stems made an excellent cooked vegetable. In the summer the cattails produced a bright golden flour which could be stored and made into pancakes and muffin-like unleavened bread. From the fall until spring time a white flour was prepared from the core of the roots. The rope-like roots crisscross just below the plant surface in great quantity. He dried them, making good flour for the winter.

There was hunting and fishing too, but everyone was doing that. The red deer, which used to be common, were now very scarce. The rabbits, the squirrels, even the fox and wolves were scarce now, and there were no fish or frogs to be caught. His little swamp was fished out by complete strangers who came and begged to fish because they were hungry.

Clo and Abt worked together, hunting and gathering food to live. They gathered mushrooms, berries, nuts, fish worms and grubs. They had several bushels of hazel nuts stored on the hut floor which they ground into a powder and mixed with the cattail flour and made pancakes. The hazel nuts attracted rats and other rodents which Abt killed, butchered and mixed with the other ingredients into a stew. It was Clo who remembered old recipes handed down from her mother and combined the gatherings with herbs and spices into tasty dishes. Abt often stood knee deep in icy water to dig out cattail roots for food. Gradually they began to live together as mates and the bond of survival had brought them together in a love of necessity.

Abt had lost his crops and had to scratch just to stay alive. He knew that the hard work in the fields had caused Ban's death and the death of his first born. He had blindly obeyed the decrees handed down by Zeff and he suffered as a result of it. The hurt lingered and festered in his heart. He would not forget it.

CHAPTER 5 THE EFRINS

An old lady bent with age was measuring handfuls of ground barley on a flat piece of slate. Beside her lay a mortar and pestle which were used to grind the barley to flour. The barley flour was about to be added to a stew for the Nese's next meal. Her face had a layer of deep tan from the weather which covered pitted pox marks. She was expressionless, almost stoic, and her motions were mechanical. The old women name was Tou and she was Pro's mother.

Dun came running to Tou, shouting, "Goot's coming and wants to see Gor." She was breathless and ruffled. "Where can I find Gor?"

Tou looked up from her work, "I believe he is in the hut." She motioned in the direction of the hut. "But why does Goot want Gor?" Gor was Tou's mate and Pro's father, he was the chief of the Nese clan, the elder statesman. Goot was the chief of the Efrin clan. The chiefs only met on special occasions which were usually elaborately prearranged. "Is something wrong? Why are they meeting, now?"

"I think he wants a potlatch. The whole clan is coming here playing symbols and drums and chanting and singing. Can you hear them?" Dun cupped her hand on her ear. "They are on their way now -- Oh, they are coming for a potlatch." A smile filled her face as she waved her hands in wild jubilation and ran off to find Gor. It was a merry get-together affair of the extended families and, Dun, age sixteen, was thoroughly caught up in the excitement.

A potlatch, mused Tou, we never have a potlatch this time of the year. Why now? It would be nice to see some friends and cousins. She shifted slowly from her crouched position Why not have a potlatch now? She smiled approvingly.

The potlatch was held after the fall equinox when both clans had harvested their crops and had gifts to give. The Nese would give grain, squash and items made of bronze. The Efrins would usually give fish from the river near their camp and special grooved pottery they made from the river clay. They would meet in an open field which was equal distance from their camp. A great bonfire would be built, straw mats were laid on the ground, food and drink would be shared and the potlatch would start. The chiefs would exchange gifts first, then the rest of the clan would participate. The purpose of the potlatch was to demonstrate that there were no warlike intentions between the two clans. The intention was to demonstrate genuine friendship. They would be dressed in their finest clothing. Goot would wear his choice skins of fox and deer. All the snarls in the fur would be combed out and it would shine in the sunlight. He always stood tall, a stately man, even thought he suffered from arthritis.

The potlatch usually was a picnic, a family reunion and a social affair where everybody celebrated the bountiful harvest.

Goot met Gor at the hut. Both men were about the same age and had been chiefs for many summer solstices. They were friends and had shared the many hardships of Stonehenge life for a long time. Gor had just been told of Goot's arrival so Gor hastily prepared two beakers of dandelion wine. He gave a glass to Goot and they toasted a greeting. Goot was dressed in loose-fitting wool clothing that was gray, the natural color of the wool. The everyday garb was a far cry from the fine attire that was worn at a potlatch. Goot bowed slightly and began, "Brother Gor, I greet you in the name of all the Efrin clan. I wish to celebrate our annual potlatch early with this gift." He presented Gor with a complete wolf's skin spread out like a rug. It was a perfect specimen, the thick black hair on the top had a translucent sheen in the sun rays. The color changed to tan and then caramel white on the underbelly and was soft to the touch.

"Potlatch? But Goot, we don't celebrate potlatch till the fall equinox. I'm not prepared for this."

"We would like to celebrate early - before the equinox. Who knows what will happen between now and the fall?"

"I don't have a fitting gift to give you -- What can I do?" Gor shrugged his shoulders.

Goot bowed his head slightly and said, "We need food." He moved towards Gor with a serious, tormented look on his face. His voice was soft and he said, "Gor, my people are starving. We have cut our meals to one a day -- and that's just a few crumbs."

Gor looked at his old friend and soon realized that the potlatch was only a charade, an excuse for a proud man to ask for help. "Of course we can give you some food, but we have very little to spare." He smiled at Goot then picked up the wolf skin and stroked the soft fur gently. He smiled and said, "Such a fine fur deserves a good potlatch exchange."

"It was a disaster this spring, the crops just did not take root and grow. So we hunted the forest and fished the river, we collected wild plants and roots and ate locusts and grubs -- anything we could find. Now we have run out of food." Goot paced back and forth in front of Gor, flailing his arms in the air at an invisible foe.

"We can give you some squashes and nuts that we have left. But, the late spring hurt us also. If it wasn't for Pro's trading for food at Cornwall we would be hungry too."

They toasted the remains of their wine. Gor said, "Come, let us tell the rest. We must prepare for the potlatch."

The Nese clansmen were preparing a normal communal meal. A large fire had been built in the center of the camp, and a huge cauldron of stew was placed in the middle of the fire. The stew consisted of goat meat with herbs, vegetables and barley flour. The Nese women were patiently stirring the soup with wooden sticks - tasting it periodically and adding measured amounts of spices and herbs. One woman was grinding particles of salt off of a large block of salt and putting it in the stew. Unleavened bread was placed on the side of the fire, warm and ready to eat. The aroma of good hot food filled the air.

The Efrins entered the camp while Gor and Goot were still at Gor's hut. They were emaciated, dressed in rags and dirty. Not in the usual attire that was worn at the potlatch. "We are here for the potlatch," said the Efrins fallaciously, avoiding eye contact with their Nese friends, instead eyeing the cauldron of stew.

"Potlatch?" questioned Tou. She raised from her crouched position and smiled broadly. "We are not ready for a potlatch. We haven't heard from Got and Goor." Then she spotted her cousin. "Fen! Fen, how are you?" Tou started towards Fen with her arms outstretched to embrace her cousin.

Suddenly the Efrins broke rank and went for the food. In a wild frenzy they pushed aside the Nese cooks and attacked the stew. Some dipped into the hot brew with cupped hands and drank. Some grabbed a leg of the goat from the pot. Some found gourd and bronze cups lying about and helped themselves to the soup. After filling themselves with food they went to every hut, tent and lean to tearing open the flaps extricating anything that got in their way - looking only for food. They threw off bone combs, sacred flint fertility statues, attractive bronze bracelets and hair pieces as they continued to search for food. Finally they found the places where more food was stored and the Efrims continued to fill themselves. They stuffed smoked rabbit and pig in their waist pouches until it fell out. They ate and played. They were jubilantly shouting, laughing and playfully throwing the food back and forth.

When the Efrims found the seed corn they were confronted by the cattle herder. "No," he shouted. "Not the seed corn - - you can't take the seed corn. We need the corn." The cattle herder went for the bag of seed corn. The Efrims simply ignored the cattle herder's plea. They danced around him and mocked him. They picked up bags of corn and threw them back and forth over his head. After the Efrins had eaten as much as they could and loaded their pouches with as much food as they could carry, they started to leave.

Before they left, some turned back, and grabbed the cattle herder and took him off as prisoner. Some of the Nese clansman shouted and pleaded with the Efrins to let the cattleman alone. The more the Nese protested the more the Efrins reacted. The Nese clansman threw clods of dirt at them and swore. One clod of dirt hit an Efrin on the shoulder; while it did not injure him, it did cause an instant response. The Efrins went back and urinated on the Nese's fire and fire wood making them useless for fuel. It added insult to injury. Then they left.

The Efrin pillage was like a lighting storm, it struck, it did great damage and then it was over as quickly as it came. The camp ground was littered with spoons, cups, bowls, stew and personal effects dragged out of the huts. Not a hut was upright. The Nese clansmen stood around staring at each other in total amazement. When Goot and Gor arrived they were awestruck, not knowing what to say. Finally Goot shouted out, "I'll be back" He shook his fist in anger and ran after the Efrins. "This is terrible! I'll be back!"

After Goot left, Gor called everyone to the camp fire in the middle of the camp.

"Let's attack them tomorrow. They can't do this to us. They took our food," shouted the beekeeper.

"They tricked us into thinking this would be a potlatch." Anger flared, fists were clenched, and tempers were hot.

"First we must determine how much food we have left," said Gor. The Nese clansman looked in every hiding place in and near the camp where food was usually stored. Some wild pig was in the stream to keep it cool. Nettle, fat hen and cleavers seeds were hung from bags in a nearby tree. Pro always brought food from Cornwall, but no one knew when Pro would be back. If he made it back in a few sunsets everything would be all right.

"Well, they didn't get it all. There is some smoked meat hanging in the tree," someone shouted from the woods.

"Yes, but they will come again and we must be prepared for a fight and drive them off," said Gor.

"Gor! Do be careful! How can we be prepared to fight without Pro?" asked Tou. She was right, the Nese numbered twenty-eight and the Efrins numbered thirty. When Pro went on his trading trips he took eight of the clan's youngest and strongest men and women. Without Pro they were vulnerable and were threatened. "The Efrins are stronger now and well fed."

"We must gather up all belongings and go to the hill camp. We will make a fort and protect ourselves." And so the Nese hill fort was started.

CHAPTER 6 THE PLAN

It had been five full moons since Pro had been Zeff's guest at Stonehenge, and now his trading party was returning from a trip in Cornwall.

Pro's party had tied his log boats securely to trees and had made camp at a familiar site along the Avon River. Everyone was in a happy mood for they were only a day's journey away from home. The skin tents were placed in a neat circle around a smoldering fire. Each tent held only two people, maybe a dog as well, but no more. There were rabbit bones, a few empty cups and some scraps of mush scattered on the ground which were the remains of the last evening meal.

In Cornwall, Pro traded for cassiterite, a brown and black gravel-like substance with a slight metallic sheen. When cassiterite is melted down, a silvery metal called tin is formed. A cargo more precious than cassiterite was hidden in dirty skin bags at the bottom of the boats. Stored beneath the cassiterite ore were bags of wheat, oats, some meat and other grains. Food! It had been a long time since the devastating snow storm, and while Pro knew his people needed food, he had no knowledge of how much.

Pro awakened early so he could prepare for the last day of his trip back to his clan. He stepped out of his tent, stretched his arms back and took a deep breath of the cool, moist morning air. His back and shoulder muscles were stiff and sore and needed a good rubbing, so he stripped off his shirt and backed into an oak tree. He moved his back up and down against the rough bark, causing some scratches between his shoulder blades, but it eased the pain of his muscles. It was something he had learned watching the bears. The sky was still black, without stars or moonlight, and the birds and other day animals were still asleep. The only exception was the eastern skyline where the sun was penetrating the darkness, creating shades of dark maroon red. As the sun rose, the colors fused into brighter shades of red which gradually blended into a red-orange hue. Finally a blazing ball of yellow fire rose, the birds began to sing, and a new day began. Pro loved the early morning before sunrise, for he knew the exact place the sun would rise in the sky. How reassuring, he thought, to know exactly where the sky goddess would rise the sun every day without fail. He thought of the unpredictable things he had seen in his travels -- the sickness, like the pox that wiped out whole clans within a full moon, uncontrolled fires that destroyed every hut in the village, people scared and maimed for life from wild animals and more. In contrast, the sun and the moon were the rock of his faith: reliable, predictable, the epitome of continuity.

How fortunate Zeff is, Pro thought. Zeff studies the sun and moon and interprets their meaning and shares his interpretation with his fellow clansman. He is so close to the movements of the sun and moon which is so important to the Stonehenge faithful. Zeff's knowledge of the heavens is unsurpassed, Pro thought. He had talked with many shaman and priests when traveling from clan to clan, but they could not compare to Zeff. Pro was proud that Zeff was now the chief priest and that he was a close friend.

Pro went to the river to wash away the grime and dirt which had accumulated from the cassiterite mines. He stripped off the remainder of his clothes and plunged in for a refreshing swim and bath. Gathering a fistful of fine sand from the river's bottom, he rubbed it on his nude body. The cold sand removed some of the body dirt and stimulated the blood flow. He scraped and rinsed several times until he felt quite clean and refreshed.

"Hey, you are making muddy water," came a shout from downstream. "What are you trying to do?"

Pro immediately recognized the voice as Qua's, and he looked beyond the shrubs on the river's edge and there was Qua, Oma and Ola bent over shallow leather bowls which they were shaking vigorously back and forth. What are they doing? Pro wondered as he walked towards them.

"You're making muddy water which gets into this food," continued Qua, chiding him gently.

Pro greeted Qua with a good morning kiss and a hug while Oma and Ola continued their work. "You know, you could simply go upstream a ways and avoid the muddy water." Pro knew the solution he had suggested was clearly obvious to all.

"Well, I know that," Qua said. "But not right now." She leaned over and kissed Pro again. "I want to see you." She smiled and pressed Pro even closer to her and they held the embrace. He kissed her on the lips and then on the neck and she smiled. He peeled off her deerskin clothing. She held him even closer as they waded into the water up to their necks where they made love.

A new day had begun with the warm sun peeking over the horizon as its children embraced in tender love. After a long moment of silence, Qua and Pro finally separated and waded back to the bank to put on their clothing. Oma and Ola were patiently waiting at the river's edge. If their parents took time to make love it meant nothing to them. In fact they would rather see them make love than argue over some small issue. "What are you doing with these bowls, Ola? Oma?" Pro asked as he finished dressing.

"Oh, we're rinsing ground acorn meal," Ola said. He presented the bowl proudly like a prize trophy. Oma presented her bowl too. The large flat wooden bowls were partially filled with water and acorn meal. They would stir the mixture with a stick, allow the meal to settle to the bottom, and then throw the cloudy water away. This panning process was repeated over and over again. "Dad, why do I have to rinse acorns anyway? Why can't I go hunting with you?"

"Yea, me too," chimed in Oma.

"We'll be home by sunset tonight, then I guess we can do some hunting tomorrow. Your grandfather and your uncle will like to hunt with us. And Oma, I'm sure your grandmother will be glad to see you." He patted her on the head. "As for the acorns, your mother mixes acorn meal with gruel and makes food." Pro looked at Qua for confirmation. She smiled and nodded. "Acorn meal is good to eat, but you must wash the bitterness out of it first. That's what you are doing for us now. You are helping prepare food for all of us in the trading party. It is important that we have good food to eat - nothing is more important than that."

Both Oma and Ola responded with a broad smile, "You are right, Dad. I never thought of it that way."

"Here, let's taste your acorn meal and see how it is." Pro dipped his finger into the white pasty mixture, held his finger out for all to see and tasted it. The twins followed their dad and did the same thing. It was bitter, very bitter and everybody cringed and spat it out immediately. "Well, you gotta get more bitterness out and it will be all right." His face was drawn and he could hardly talk.

"Dad? Why do I have to go to Stonehenge and train to be a priest?" asked Ola. "I wanta go with you and Mom and trade at Cornwall."

"Yeah, if Ola goes to Stonehenge, I want to go with him, too," pleaded the other twin. "But, no, I really want to stay with you."

The twins ran over to Pro and tugged at his sleeve. "I want to stay here with you and Mom. - I don't want to train with Zeff and his old white deer skin. Can I stay? Can I, Dad? I'll rinse all the acorn meal that you want me to. You won't have to tell me, either."

"Yeah. Me too. I want to stay with you," pleaded Oma.

Pro placed the acorn meal down between the twins and glanced at Qua with a troubled look. "Well, I don't know. It is an honor to become a priest at Stonehenge." He rubbed his ear and again glanced at Qua, but she looked away. "You won't be old enough to go to Stonehenge for a few summer solstices - so it is too soon to talk about now.-- So, then, the first meal will be gruel?" Pro turned to Qua.

"Yes, we will use the blood from the deer, organ meat mixed with acorn paste, wild parsnips and yellow goatsbread. That's what we will have for our rations."

"Yes, but you missed the best ingredients of them all, didn't she?" Pro asked. "Well, it's spices. You have a magic bag of spices that you use to make the gruel taste special. Don't deny it. I've tasted many good rations and I know." Pro smiled.

"Well, yes." She smiled back. "I haven't decided exactly what I'll use, but we have wild garlic and others."

Suddenly the camp dogs jumped to their feet, cocked their ears back and burst out in loud barking. Everyone immediately stopped what they were doing, picked up their spears, and stood in readiness. Pro's party could see very little for the visibility was screened out by the thick green foliage. The dogs were their sentry and first warning against any unseen enemy hidden in the forest. Finally, off in the distance, someone came slashing through the thicket towards them.

"Who is it?" Jep sputtered. He was awake now as were the rest of the party.

"I don't know." Pro was puzzled as the noise became louder. "I wonder if there is just one person? He certainly isn't sneaking up on us like a pack of wolves on a deer." Pro rubbed a scar on his chin which tingled when he became nervous. "He is making so much noise we could hear him without the dogs."

Qua observed, "That he is a she, and it looks like she is hurt. She is staggering towards us. Over here," she shouted. "We can help you, over here." Qua was always the first to help anyone, to give what medicine she had from herbs and shrubs she carried in her waist pouch. It was a wonderful attribute, and Pro respected her for it, but it was also dangerous.

Pro was more cautious. "This could be a trick, Qua. Let her come a little closer before we help. We could be ambushed from the rear easily while she has our attention." Pro noticed that the dogs were facing the approaching woman and Pro wondered if they would detect someone sneaking up from the back. "Jep, keep your eye on the rear side of us for any suspicious movement." Jep did as he was told. The thrashing about of brush became louder and a woman stumbled into the camp site.

"Dun! It's Dun from our own Nese clan," shouted Qua. Her deer skin clothing was ripped and torn to shreds and her upper torso was scratched by thorns, and blood was smeared over her body. She ran to the camp fire and collapsed on the ground at Qua's feet. Exhausted!

Qua examined Dun and determined that her lacerations were minor cuts caused when she ran through blackberry bushes. Qua promptly got some water and gave it to Dun to sprinkle on the cuts and scratches. She dipped a piece of a puff ball mushroom and used it as gauze. "Sit down over here, honey." Qua put a soft sheep skin over a log and made it inviting for her.

"Food, I need food. I'm so hungry. Can I have something to eat?"

"Why yes, of course, you can have the first meal with us. Yes, we were just talking about that," Pro mumbled. "We are glad to see you, Dun." He turned and called, "Jep, we are not being attacked." Then he motioned to the others to help Ola and Oma speed up the preparation of the acorn meal. He wanted to help her but he didn't know how. Finally he offered her a piece of flat, unleavened biscuit he carried in his pouch. "Here, eat this for now." She ate the biscuit in two big bites and licked her fingers when she was done. Pro stepped back with his hands on his hips wondering what had happened to Dun. She was always flirting with other men. Had she gotten in trouble? He didn't know how to tactfully ask her what was wrong and why she was here.

"Don't go into our village." Dun blurted out. "I beg you. Don't go. They will rob you. They may even kill you," she pleaded in breathy staccato sounds.

"Rob? Kill? I don't understand. We just want to come home after a long trip," Pro said. "What really happened?"

Dun told the full story of the Efrin attack "They have even taken my father," she said. She looked up at Pro and began to sob. "They have taken my father prisoner and they won't return him unless we give them grain and our cattle." She embellished the truth slightly, her talk was interrupted by gasps for air. Pro motioned for Qua to come and comfort her. When she got control of herself, she continued, leaning over as if saying something confidential. "I can't blame them. They have nothing to eat in their village. Nothing!" She gulped hard and continued. "They are so thin and desperate looking. Their children have sunken gray eyes and they are all sick." She paused, straightened up to her full stature and said, "The Efrins were good people. In the past we used to trade and even choose mates with them. My cousin was an Efrin, and so is my uncle Fib, and he is a good man. They just have nothing to eat, and they raided us for food. It is terrible." Pro had to admire Dun. Her father, the cattleman, was captured by the Efrins, yet she was understanding, even magnanimous.

Pro was beginning to put the story together now. He had been gone many full moons getting tin and did not know how devastating the crop failure in the spring had been. His clan seldom had people starving. In fact, the Stonehenge farmers always had enough food and cattle for themselves, and would give extras to the Stonehenge shrine. The villagers would steal wives and dogs, once in a while, but never food. "You mean that the Efrins are so starved and desperate for food that they were driven to raiding - and even worse?" Pro questioned.

"Yes. We used to have a potlatch and feasts with the Efrins. We never went to their village and they never came to ours. We just met in a field and exchanged gifts. Our chief, your father, Gor, and their chief always competed to see who could exchange the biggest gifts. Do you remember?" asked Dun.

Pro nodded. "My father - Gor, where is he? And my mother and brother, are they safe?"

"They are safe. Gor went north in the hills with the clan before they came the second time."

"The second time!? You mean they raided twice." The story got worse and Dun did not correct the misleading exaggeration. She paused, caught her breath and continued, "My father was taken and he is sick, too. Very sick."

"Your father sick? How sick?" Pro asked.

"He was spitting up blood and it wouldn't go away. He felt dizzy and needed to lie down to rest often. Then he felt better, for awhile, and then the Efrins came and took him away." Though stoicism was an inherent virtue among her people, she could not hold back her tears and she sobbed and shivered.

Jep sat down beside Dun and gently hugged her, "Your father is a brave man, Dun," Jep said. He examined Dun's cuts and found that they had stopped bleeding and had been wiped clean. Jep took off his jacket and placed it around her shoulders. He put a woolen sheep skin over her legs and sat closer to her to keep her warm. She was at ease, now, and smiled weakly for the first time.

Pro, although the mighty and able leader of his clan, was always the last one to know about any romances among his people. His wife said he could spot a red deer in heat at a hundred paces but couldn't spot a clan romance at two. Pro glanced at Qua under an arched eyebrow and shrugged his shoulders. He just hadn't expected the strange behavior between Jep and Dun. Qua smiled to herself, for she had been watching them for some time and she knew. "How did you know we would be camped here?" she asked.

"Jep told me," Dun replied.

"Jep? How did Jep know we would be camped here?"

"Jep said that you always camp here just before you come home. I've come out here every sun rise for the past five sun rises to warn you." She looked at Pro like a trusting and innocent child.

"Well, I guess that's right." Pro paused. "About your father, we are truly grateful to him." He was familiar with the symptoms of Dun's father's sickness and knew there were few who lived through it. Victims gradually became so weak that they died. It appeared that Dun's father had sacrificed himself for the clan. He had prevented the impetuous kidnapping of the women and further destruction of the village. "Yes, Dun, your father was a very brave man, and we shall never forget him." He wanted to give her something to show his gratitude, so he rummaged through his waist pouch and found his last piece of smoked deer meat. It was something that he personally liked to munch on, so he brushed off the bits of dirt and gave it to her. Dun accepted it with a gracious smile and ate it.

"When the Efrins left," Dun continued, "Gor decided to post some men outside our village to watch for them. Meanwhile, we packed everything of value and moved before they came again." Dun, now, had everyone's attention so she continued to embellish the facts, slightly. "When they came the third time, there was little in the village for them to take. Everything of value had been taken up in the hills. Oh, we left some food behind for them to find.-- just enough so they wouldn't follow us to the hills." A slight smile creased across Dun's mouth. "When the Efrins found out that there was nobody at the village, they tore it down and left."

"I can't believe it!" Pro stood up from his crouched sitting position and began swinging his arms around in wild gestures. He picked up a clod of clay and threw it against a tree as hard as he could, breaking it into a hundred pieces. "I just can't believe it!" He stopped swinging momentarily and questioned Dun again. "Are the other clans raiding and stealing like the Efrins?"

"Oh, yes!" Dun shook her head, her forehead wrinkled. "It's bad, real bad! There is no food in the land towards the sun set." She pointed to the west. "There are at least four clans that are starving and may be raiding others by now."

Stunned, Pro sat down on the log and buried his head in his hands. He mumbled, "Dogs, snakes" and a few other obscenities. Jep, Qua, and the rest of the trading party gathered close by and sat on their knees and waited. Their proximity was assurance to Pro that whatever he decided, they would be with him. Pro sat in silence for at least a half hour, just thinking.

Jep broke the silence. "We are here to help. Let us help."

Pro raised his head and said, "I know, I know. You all are ready to help, and it will take all of us. Believe me." He stood up to his full height. "Come, let's make some plans." They went to the river's edge where there was an area of smooth sand along the bank. He took a stick and drew "X" marks and lines in the sand. "This is where we are, at the fork in the river, and this is where the Nese clan is in the hills. The

Efrins are on the sun set of the river between us and our clan. We must get through with our food and supplies without the Efrins stopping us."

"They would kill us for the food alone," said Jep. There was a silent pause as everyone exchanged incredulous glances. The Efrins had Pro's party outnumbered three to one and they could easily wipe out his men and steal the food. .

"We've got the boats filled with cassiterite so we'll have to travel by river," said Jep. "How can we get past the Efrins?" He jabbed a stick in the sand map where the Efrins were camped.

"Nothing is easy, Jep. It would take too much time to unload the boats and carry the tin over the hills to our clan," said Pro.

"We don't have the men either," said Jep with a sigh, glancing at the eight log boats loaded to the top with heavy ore.

"Any clan would be desperate enough to attack when they are starving," added Dun. "In fact, probably the best thing is to attack them first before they attack us. Just stop them before they hurt us."

Pro was taken aback by Dun's casual remark. The more he thought about it, the more he favored attacking the Efrins and taking charge, but not now.

"How can we get past the Efrins along the river bank?" asked Jep.

A plan was developing in Pro's head "Just wait till nightfall." Pro looked at Jep, and a confident smile came over his face. "Yes, just wait till it's black tonight. We'll stay here all day and move up the river tonight." Several of the clansman jumped up from their hunched over position and shouted,

"No - noo, we can't go out in the black of night. The werewolves, Pro. They would catch us and kill us," someone protested. The party was visibly disturbed and there was mumbling and grumbling from all quarters.

Pro rose to his feet and stood on a slightly elevated patch of ground. "Werewolves? Have you ever seen a werewolf? I haven't and you haven't either. We've never seen a werewolf in all the times we have been traveling to Cornwall. And we have spent many nights under the stars. We are afraid of the blackness, something we think is there but never is. That is why we take dogs on our trips to Cornwall. They can tell us what is in the blackness."

"I still don't like it," mumbled Jep.

"We don't have any choice, Jep. If we stay here, the Efrins will attack our clan at the hill fort, and they have Gor outnumbered and they will win. Then they will come and find us. Again they would have our party outnumbered and they will win. If we travel by daylight they can easily overtake us. We must be brave and move tonight."

CHAPTER 7 THE PERILOUS JOURNEY

There was a loud splash. "Oh, ooh!" Pro yelled. He had lost his balance and was swirling down in the river water. "Quiet, Pro, shh," said Jep.

Pro had just slipped on a smooth submerged stone covered with green slimy moss which angled down sharply into deep water. He swam past the deep spot and found solid footing as fast and as silently as he could. Pro peered across the river at the two Efrin guards sitting around their beach fire. . .

"What was that?" yelled the emaciated Efrin guard as he stopped stirring the fire with a stick. They were lying around a beach fire absorbing the heat and engrossed in the dancing flames.

"I don't know," answered the second. "Listen." He cupped his ear in the direction of the noise. They both rose to their feet and looked across the river, seeing a blurry curtain of leaves from low hanging willow trees.

"You know what I think it was?" asked the first. "I think it was a big bass a'floppin in the water. You know there is a big bass hole over there."

"Oh, yeah? ... Ha. I think you are dreaming. This river's been all fished out. There's no more fish in this river.. and you know it."

"Well, what was it then?" He wet his finger and held it in the air. "There's no breeze a'blowin. No air at all. What could cause that noise?"   The guards paused and continued looking at the willow trees across the river. The night was black and chilly, and the only light came from their blazing beach fire. Elongated yellow and orange reflections fluttered across the water and then disappeared. The river was as black as tar and moved along in a gentle continuous flow, slapping now and then against the shore.

"I don't know, and I don't really want to know." The second guard shrugged his shoulders.

"What else would it be if it isn't a fish?"

The guard thought for a moment. "You know how big it would have been to make that much noise?" He held his hand about two feet apart. "That big."

"Yeah, I know. And you know what, at daylight why don't we get a boat and catch us that fish?" He leaned over, held his hand to his mouth and whispered.

"Yeah -- don't tell anyone about it, either. We can take it to the other side of the river, build a fire and eat it ourselves." The men hadn't had a good meal in several full moons and the idea of having as much as they wanted for themselves had a commanding appeal. They smiled approvingly at each other, then stretched out on the sand around the fire.

We're safe for a while, Pro thought. His caravan was wading in water up to their chests towing eight ore boats. Behind him was Jep, Qua, Ola, Oma and the rest of the party, each pulling or pushing the cargo along. They were as close to the eastern bank of the river as they could get. Overhead was a canopy of branches from weeping willow trees which stretched down to the water's edge. Underneath they sliced their way through cattail and other swamp plants along the river bank. The concealment was excellent, but the mosquitoes were practically unbearable. Finally they smeared their hands, faces and hair with thick layers of black mud from the bottom of the river. The pasty mud had a putrid odor of rotten eggs and was slimy to the touch. It was terrible, but it worked. Not only did it discourage the mosquitoes, but the camouflage blended into the black night like a shadow.

"Oops. Splash! Oh!" came a loud cry. Someone else in the caravan had stepped on the slimy stone and slipped off as Pro had. This noise was even louder than before. Two loud noises so close together would surely attract attention, Pro thought. The guards would probably wake the rest of the clan and come to investigate. If they did, should we abandon the boats and hide in the thicket along the bank? What if we were caught? Everyone stopped dead still and stood in a crouched position facing the Efrins. Their eyes fixed on the guards' every move.

The first guard stretched his arms to their full extent and then yawned. "There it is again."

"Must really be a big one. I can hardly wait till daybreak." He stretched out on the sandy beach to move away from the hot fire.

"I can hardly wait, too. I'm so hungry I could eat grass."

"The starvin is really bad now. You know Stom's mate died in childbirth today? The baby, too. She was too weak. Neither of them had a chance." He shook his head. "Not a chance."

"I know, I know." He shook his head. "It's terrible."

"This is all that priest at Stonehenge's fault, you know? He told everybody to start plantin' too early, and the snow storm killed the plants before they got started."

"You shouldn't talk about the high priest that way! He knows what he is doin. He gets a sign from the sun and moon."

"Do you know what we should do? We should get a boat and go catch that bass and eat it tonight."

The second guard stared at his friend and thought for a moment. He stirred the fire with a stick and uncovered some cherry red coals. Then he jumped to his feet and said, "Let's do it. We can wrap it up in big leaves and cook it on this fire and no one will ever know. Come on, let's go." They kicked a little wet sand to reduce the fire and ran down to the far end of the beach where the boats were tied.

The guards were running in the opposite direction of the noise and Pro couldn't determine why. They had abandoned their post and left the entire river front unguarded. He knew that now was the time to move his party out of trouble. The coverage from the overhanging trees and cattails stopped just ahead. They had reached a stretch of white sandy beach about one hundred paces wide. It was a crescent-shaped lagoon with shallow water extending into the river. They would be completely exposed when they crossed that section.

Pro looked back at the caravan of boats. Oma was riding across the deep hole by clinging to the side of the boat which allowed her to be pulled to surer footing. That's my intelligent daughter, thought Pro with a proud smile.

When the caravan got ready to cross the white sand bar, Pro motioned for Jep and the others to come to him. "I've got a plan," he whispered. He pulled out a section of leather rope long enough to reach across the sand bar area twice. "I'll tie one end of this rope to the boat and you hold on to the other end. I'll take the rope with me across the sand bar. I'll have to swim underwater, as quietly as I can, to the thick coverage on the other side of the sand bar," he pointed. "When I get to the other side I'll pull the boats slowly across the exposed water. Jep, you pull the other end of the rope back and tie it to the next boat. We'll keep doing this until we get all eight boats across. If the Efrins notice the boats, they will think they are just floating logs."

"Which they are," added Jep. "From the distance they look like an old log floating down the river."

"That's right," Pro said. "Now let's make it work. After we get the first two boats pulled over, the rest of you take your turn and swim underwater to the thicket." Everyone nodded agreement. "Shh, no more talk." Pro put his finger to his lips.

The guards had gathered two wooden sticks and two bone fish hooks and were putting them into their boat. One stopped and stood up straight like a ramrod. "What was that?" He cupped his ear to listen. "It sounded like someone talkin'."

The second guard noticed his friend stopped working with the fishing line and stood upright too. "I didn't hear anything. All kinds of sounds carry across the water, you know."

"I know that, but it sounded like voices."

The second guard looked at the motionless silent river. "Now you're the one dreamin'. Heck, we're so hungry we're both a - dreamin'."

"But it did sound like someone a talkin'. Way down the river there." He pointed towards the sand bar. "I think we should see what it is."

"Could have been a raccoon washin his food."

"Raccoons don't talk. We should see what it is. Could be something dangerous."

"It could be anythin'. Night animals come to the river always a makin' noises." He moved the fishing sticks to the edge of the boat. "You are so bloody hungry that you hear the river talkin'. It could be an owl or frog. Who knows what? All I know is that I'm hungry and I'm goin to catch me a fish."

"No, I think it was someone talkin'."

Again the second guard scanned the river surface from shore line to shore line. "Now I don't see anything out there." he said. "But if you want to go out and look, let's go."

"I think we should, just to be sure."

"But let's take our fishin' poles along so we can do some fishin' too."

"Yes. I guess so."

The second guard opened a leather box where fishing bait was kept. "Where's the bait?"

"Oh, there is no bait. We ate it all days ago."

"No bait? We'll have to roll over some rocks and find our own grubs."

"Do you think we can find any bait in the dark?"

"I don't know, but let's try." They left their boat and began to look under rocks and logs for bait. They found none, not because it was too dark to see, but because most of the rocks and logs had been rolled over days before and the grubs and worms were eaten by other hungry clansmen.

One by one the log boats slowly and silently crossed the exposed waterway without being noticed. Then they picked their way along the east bank tripping over unseen rocks and submerged logs, but they knew they were safe as they distanced themselves from the Efrins. By late afternoon they arrived at the Nese fort.

CHAPTER 8 THE FAMILY MEETING

Tou was scraping a piece of deer skin with the sharp edge of flint a blade. The piece of flint was small with practically no handle to grip, but it had a surgically sharp edge. One slight error could result in serious injury. She was rubbing particularly hard over a knotted section of cartilage that refused to be separated from the hide. She sprinkled water on the skin from a gourd to soften the knotted spot. Special care was required to avoid cutting a hole through the hide. Large, complete pieces of the hide were protection against the winter winds, while a hide with even a small hole would be drafty. She was working and waiting.

"They are here. They are here. The trading party is back," someone called out. Tou stopped scraping, washed her hands in clean water and wiped them on her skirt. She ran to meet the trading party as fast as her weary bones could carry her.

"Pro, Pro, are you all right?"

"Yes, Ma, I'm all right. I'm coming."

A smile appeared on her face accompanied by a sigh of relief. She slowed her pace a bit for fear of falling, and Gor appeared from a shed and said, "Wait for me," and they ran together.

"And Qua and Ola and Oma, are they all right?"

"Yes, yes, Dad, mom. We made it safely to the fort."

A breathless mother pressed her last son close to her bosom, glad that he was back. She remembered when her little boy was only three summer solstices old and was seriously burned. He was chasing a feather when he tripped and tumbled into a camp fire. A hot coal was pressed into his chin and left a scar the size and shape of a dandelion blossom. In one fluid motion she had grabbed him and run to the river to cool the burn. She had saved his life and she hugged him then as she was hugging him now, glad that he was safe and alive.

"We are so happy that you are back. So thankful," she gasped. "Some thought you would not return. Some thought you would go to the old village where the Efrin would attack you. How did you know to come to the fort?" Pro told her how Dun had come to the camp at the river's fork and warned them. She gulped hard and gave Pro an extra tight squeeze as tears began to well in her eyes.

Everyone in the trading party was hugging and greeting each other like family. Qua made her way through the crowd to Pro's mother and embraced her. She whispered in her ear, "The fertility god has been good to us. I am expecting a child."

"Does Pro know about it yet?"

"No; I will tell him after we have celebrated with the clan."

All the families of the trading party came and cried tears of joy. Little children jumped up and down, asking questions of Pro's party. It was a time to be happy and renew old ties, for Pro had been gone three full moons, an unusually long time. Some of the Nese clan had written them off completely. It was not uncommon for trading parties to disappear without a trace.

Mott, Pro's older brother, welcomed everyone with generous portions of mead and wine. There would be time to talk about the desperately hungry Efrins and other starving clans later.

"The biggest red deer that I could get has been killed," declared Gor. "We will feast tonight."

The deer was vigorously attacked by a team of women, each with a given task. The hide was carefully removed and saved. The blood was collected in leather bowls and set aside for another day's meal. The liver would be roasted and eaten by the honored leaders. All the inner organs were saved for later. Even the large penis was cut off and became a prop in a ritual dance that evening.

The children raced down to the stream where they fetched leather bowls that had been soaking. The water swelled the seams of the bowls together so they would hold liquids. Sheep and goat bladders were filled with mead and wine and were placed in the stream to cool.

Meanwhile, the clan fire-maker had added more wood to the fire to prepare for the roast. He had carefully selected long dead limbs from the forest floor because he was not allowed to use the wood he had chopped days before. He didn't know why. Chopping new logs for fire wood with flint axes was a tedious and time consuming job, so he made a "star" fire by extending the long limbs from his fire in every direction. As the fire burned down, he would feed the extended logs into the hot coals. The whole operation looked like a huge starfish spread on the beach. The body was the fire and the arms were the dry logs ready to be pushed as needed. Rising up from the fire was blue-gray smoke and the musty aroma of burning oak wood. The wood was dry, and cracking and snapping easily as the coals were built up for cooking.

The fire-maker was good at his task, and he coaxed Jep to join him. As they worked together they began singing a well known hunting song. Jep's monotone sounded worse than a sick crow, so he joined the merriment by weaving his head back and forth with the melody and occasionally grunting some words. The women sang also while preparing the deer. The singing was contagious, and everyone joined in as work and pleasure went hand in hand.

The fire-maker had to make a wood spit long enough to extend across the fire and strong enough to hold the large deer over the coals. The spit, itself, could not catch on fire and burn. Green wood was considered sacred and could not be used because it contained sap and was still alive with the vital juice from the fertility god. To destroy something which a god had ordained to live was sacrilegious.

They prevented the wooden spit from burning by soaking dead wood in the stream allowing it to absorb water. Three sturdy oak limbs had been especially chosen, and two of them had a 'V' shaped crotch at one end. The third was the cross beam which would be stuck through the deer from head to anus. The limbs had been anchored in the stream some distance from the fort. "Jep, let's you and me fetch the wood for the spit, eh?" said the fire-maker.

"I'll be glad to," said Jep. "But I know they will be heavy, for they have been a'soakin for a long time." Off they went.

When they got to the stream they saw a strange man standing on a rock, splashing his bare feet in the water. Jep and the fire-maker approached the man quietly from behind and then stood unnoticed for a moment. The man commenced to splash himself with cool water and then laughed as he shivered while drying himself. He threw a flat stone across the water and watched it skip. He tried it again and succeeded in skipping the stones a few more times. Then he giggled like a little child. "That's a good throw." Smeared on the shore stones were the remains of frogs, tadpoles and crawdads that he had eaten. The wraparound, trouser-like pants were torn into streaks of rags and he wore no shirt. His pants had large spots of greasy dirt on the front. He repeated skipping stones several times.

Finally Jep lowered his spear in readiness and yelled, "Who are you?" His voice boomed out in the silence and the startled stranger turned suddenly, slipped on a rock, made an awkward flip in the air and fell into the stream with a loud splash.

Jep and the fire-maker laughed out loud and approached the stranger. "I know who he is," said the fire-maker. "He's an Efrin looking for food."

"Maybe we should take him back to the fort and see what Pro wants to do with him."

"Yeah, he could help carry these heavy split logs too."

They ate well. They also drank well, and everyone had a merry time. The entire clan sat around the fire and talked into the night. They loved hearing how Pro's party slipped by the Efrin guards under the hanging willow branches and Pro told how they swam underwater and pulled their boats past the white sandy beach. The children and adults alike all cheered and laughed, and it was long after dark when they all went to sleep.

Hovering over their exuberance like a black storm cloud was the terrible threat from the Efrins. The Efrins had been a brother clan for many summer solstices, and now they were desperately hungry and had become a threat.

CHAPTER 9 BRONZE

The hilltop settlement of the Nese clan was different from the one in the valley. Circled around the edge of the hill was a log palisade fence about six feet high with pointed tops and about a hundred paces in diameter. Inside the settlement were three circular, timber-framed huts with thatched roofs. Gor and Tou lived in the main dwelling in the center of the fort. Mott and his woman lived in the smaller one. The third hut was set up for smelting tin and copper. The rest of the clan lived in huts outside the palisade where they farmed their plots of ground. Gor and Mott were showing Pro around the encampment.

"Do you think you are safe from the Efrins here?" Pro asked.

"We hope so. If the Efrins attack, everyone, women, children, everyone would come into the stockade and bring their livestock." He pointed to pens of cattle, pigs, sheep and goats inside the fort. "We will fill up the pens and close the gate when we are under attack."

"The Efrins are savage, unpredictable like a wild boar," observed Mott. "If they attack the fort, they will have to come up the hill to get us. From this vantage point, we will always be firing arrows down at them from behind our log walls."

"They could come at night and burn the fields, couldn't they?" Pro asked.

"Yes, but they haven't. Burning the fields is destroying food. I -- I just can't see them doing that." Gor uttered weakly. His hand shook when he thought about the tragic situation. His arthritic ankles hurt when he walked, so he limped to a rock in the middle of the fort where he sat. "I can't walk around the fort with you, Pro. My joints hurt so and my teeth, they hurt too." He rubbed his teeth with his finger. They were almost all gone, and those that he had were blackened.

"Oh, I'm sorry, Pa." It was hard for Pro to realize that his father was old and in need of rest. He had always been in control and the driving force in the clan. Pro was shocked, for he had never thought that his father would have to slow down. "I hope that you feel better soon." He glanced at Mott. Somehow both knew that Gor wouldn't get better. His hair was gray and his eyes were dim and moist. He was an old man bent with age. Who had been on the earth 39 summer solstices.

"Let me show you some of the things we have saved from the valley. We have melting pots for making bronze and we have two new bellows made of goat skin." He managed a smile through all his discomfort.

"Good, Pa, I'm glad to hear that. But listen to what I've learned." Pro motioned for Mott and his father to move closer. "I've learned a new way of making bronze from the merchants at Cornwall. It's done with beeswax."

"Beeswax?" questioned Mott. "Beeswax!?" Mott could not believe what he heard. "Pro, I think you have been under the full moon with the women too much." Both laughed. "You know how the full moon affects the women?" They all laughed. Mott was referring to the fertility rite of the full moon where the younger women would meet at the clan's "earth ring" and strip off their clothes. After dancing and chanting, they would lie naked with their legs spread apart facing the full moon. The light of the moon was believed to give them a magic power to become pregnant. Many times young men in the clan would participate in the rite, and an amazing number of the women, in fact, became pregnant. Thus, the romantic effect of the full moon was always popular.

"Get me some beeswax and I'll show you."

The bee keeper was summoned and some beeswax was obtained. "You make a model of the spear head or ax or whatever you want. Like this." He stretched out the wax on a sheet of clay. Where the wax was thick, he placed his warm hand until it became soft and pliable. Pro cut away excess wax from around the edges with a knife and molded and shaped the wax until he had the exact shape he wanted. He presented the finished model to Mott. "This is called a leaf-shaped sword." The completed strip was shaped with a narrow blade and handle and was about 18 inches long. On the handle he drew grip marks. The wax was made smooth by spitting on his hands and rubbing the rough edges down. For his finishing touch, he tapered the point, making it sharper. "Do you see, Mott?"

Mott drew closer and stared at the wax. He laughed again. "Do you know what I see? I see the form of a sword carved out of beeswax lying on a slate of clay. You call this a sword?" He smiled, "I really do think that you have spent too much time under the full moon with the maidens."

"Oh, I'm not finished. Then you put molding clay around the wax model. Now you bake it. The mold hardens and the wax melts and you pour it out. Then you pour hot bronze into the mold, let it cool, break open the clay and you have your sword."

"And you save the beeswax for something else," added the father.

Mott's creative mind was working. "You can make practically anything out of the soft beeswax, can't you?"

"Yes." Pro smiled. "Yes, you can. I knew you would like this, Mott. There is something else. You can use the wax over and over and make daggers and spears and as many weapons as you want."

Mott had made a special area in the stockade to mix the copper and tin together. He had supervised making the fire places where the molten bronze would be made, and he was ready to start making bronze immediately.

"Good, Pro, you bring valuable news to us," said Gor, proud of his son's contribution to the clan. He pointed. "Look, over there is a huge pile of dry dead wood cut for a fire." He smiled, "I've been saving it for your coming with the cassiterite. I wouldn't even let the fire-maker use it for the deer last night."

"Now I have some news for you, too," Mott said. "We have gathered all the old copper that we could find in that pile over there." He pointed. "If we melt ten parts copper to one part cassiterite, we will make better bronze than melting copper ore. It's purer and makes better bronze." No one knew why when you combined tin and copper together you got bronze a metal harder and stronger than either tin or copper.

"Good," Pro said. He nodded his head in approval. "We are strong! We are strong! Think of all the swords and spears we can make. We will have the best weapons to fight with, so let's attack the Efrins and get it over with."

The three men agreed and shouted in unison, "We are strong! We are strong!" Mott and Pro did a little dance, but Gor stopped participating. He raised his hand to halt the celebration. The men became silent. He sat back on the rock and calmly asked, "Pro, how much food did you bring?"

Pro held up ten fingers. "It's bags of wheat mostly, which we should use for seed. It is good enough to keep for seed."

"We need it for food, now - you can get more for seed later," Gor said, mustering as much forcefulness as he could. "The Efrins are desperate and they need food now! It is the only way that we can stop them from attacking us!"

Pro's face turned serious and he nodded his head in silent agreement. "Think about this. First, we have food, enough of it. And second, we can make superior spears and swords with beeswax molds. We can kill anybody who tries to fight us and we can control these people. I think that we should attack the Efrins first."

Gor stood up on his wobbly feet and a confident smile radiated through the pain on his face. "We will make it," he said. Gor then became serious and looked directly at both his sons, "But we will feed the Efrins first and only fight them if we have to." He paused. "They have been our neighbors for more summer solstices than I can remember. They still would be friends if they weren't starving. It is not right to consider the Efrins an enemy when we can save them by bringing them food even though they have attacked us. We can settle with them about the damage they have done us after we have fed them."

Thus the issue was settled.

By now the clan workers noted the cheering and stopped their work. The herders, the leather workers and all traders stopped and joined in the cheering. The women stopped working too and cheered. They sensed that something good had happened, but they had no idea what. The celebration was short lived as Gor said, "We must reach the Efrins today with food."

"Is Goot still their leader?" Pro asked.

"I don't know. Maybe this Efrin they found by the river can tell us that." Gor motioned with his hand, and one of his men summoned the Efrin.

The Efrin wore a contented smile because he had a full belly. He had been treated not as a prisoner, but as a friend in need. This was a risk. If the rest of the Efrins found out how much food the Nese had, they would surely raid again.

"What's your name?" asked Gor.

"Hal." He shifted uneasily from one foot to the other.

"I want to ask you some questions. How is Goot?"

"Goot? Goot is dead. He died and the spirit left him. Like so many of my people."

Gor was shocked at first, then he realized that many of his old friends would be dead from the famine. "When did he die?"

"About two sunsets ago."

"Who's the new chief?"

"Don't need one. We're all dying from hunger."

Again Gor was surprised. "How many people are alive at your village?"

"Maybe twenty, maybe less, but they are all lying around, sick and dying."

"You mean that they are all too weak to move about?"

"They're lying around dying."

Gor turned to Pro. "If he's telling the truth, we can take them food without any danger."

"I believe he is. Why would he lie about this?" Pro said. He turned to Hal. "If you are telling the truth, then we want to take food to your people. If you are lying, and your people turn on us, you will die the slowest death known."

"They are too weak to fight. Why would they fight you if you are bringing food? I'll go with you and you can see."

Everyone nodded in agreement. "You take the people from your trading party and your food to the Efrins." Gor told Pro. "We'll feed them until they are strong, and then the Efrins can pay us back -- somehow. Mott, you stay here and make bronze," He motioned for the Efrin to be taken away, then added with a cautionary comment. "We'll do it with a sentry like the crows."

"The crows?" Pro puzzled. "Oh, yes, that's right, safe like the crows." One of the womenfolk would watch from the woods and see what the Efrins do. If the Efrins started any trouble she would run to the fort and the rest of the Nese clan would come to the rescue.

"Sentry, just like the crows," toasted Mott.

"Like the crows," chimed in Gor and Pro.

CHAPTER 10 BLESSED ARE THE PEACE MAKERS

Though Pro had been warned, he did not expect the sickening conditions he found, for the village was completely void of human activity. The only sound was the ruffle of the wind through the leaves of the willow trees along the river's edge and the occasional ripple in the river. Usually the arrival of strangers was heralded by dogs barking and excited children stirring about. There was none of that. Bones of goats and sheep were strung out haphazardly along the river bank, void of all meat and bleached white from the sun.

Pro walked over to the fire site, pushed the charred logs around with his foot and looked up at Hal. "The fire-maker has allowed the fire to die out?!" The fire provided heat to cook by and the only light in the night time. Allowing a fire to go out was a very serious matter, and fire-makers had been executed by their clan members for such carelessness.

Hal went to the fire site and felt the logs with his hands. They were cold. "He had been sick; I guess he couldn't make the fire anymore."

"And no one could help him keep the fire going?" questioned Pro.

"I guess not."

The absence of a fire was a clear indication that the Efrins were a dying people, at least sickened to the extent of not being able to care about essential things. Pro surveyed the campsite and found that no fire wood had been cut and laid aside. He found broken bowls, pottery, flint tools, knives and flint axes scattered over the ground. Flies covered the skeletal remains of rats, raccoons, birds and other unidentified creatures. The Efrins' fishing boats apparently hadn't been used for days and were on the shore bottom up with cracks in their hulls from the hot sun.

A golden plover, a bird that eats carrion, circled and lit on the hull of one the boats. It jumped to the ground looking for insects, worms or scraps of carrion to eat and found none. The mournful and sober song of the golden plover sounded distinct and clear, for there was no other sound of nature for it to blend with. It was a fateful prelude to a funeral service. The bird flew away.

At first Pro thought the Efrins were hiding in their huts and feared a senseless sunrise attack. Pro approached Hal. "Hal, see if anyone is alive in the huts and get them to come out, if they can." Hal went from hut to hut, and presently emaciated figures emerged like walking zombies. They were ghost-like and expressionless, slow to respond to offers of food.

"Here, take some wheat meal," Jep offered. Slowly, hesitantly, the Efrin emerged and took food. They ate little bits at a time, staring back in disbelief. Soon they realized that there really was food and that this was not another disappointing dream. They ate more and more and gradually their faces transformed into smiles and they began to talk among each other. The Efrins would have eaten more food and probably gotten very sick if it hadn't been for Jep. "It isn't good for them to eat too much so soon," he said.

"Why? Why not give them as much food as they can eat? They certainly need it," Pro protested.

"No, no. I remember when the Maron clan had the flood that washed away all their food and they were starving. Some got deathly sick when they ate too much, too soon. Wait till tomorrow. You have to go slowly with them." Jep's recollection was correct, for some of the Maron clan had overeaten and had even died because their bellies were not ready for large quantities of food.

The water from the river wasn't fit to drink, although water was needed desperately. Pro had the men gather wood and prepare fires. They filled the bronze bucket and heated enough water for everyone. As the water boiled, Pro mixed crushed dried dandelion roots into the water and the brew turned brown in color. When it cooled everyone drank Pro's favorite elixir which he believed had great healing powers.

Every method of obtaining food had been tried by the Efrins and still there was not enough to eat. All the dogs had been eaten and they were deemed essential for protection from night attack by animals or man. There was no livestock in the pens where goats, cattle and pigs had been kept. The foot prints of various animals in the mud and manure had hardened long ago from the sun, forming grotesque shapes. What was once a food source and a mark of status to the livestock owner was now a cruel reminder of what had been lost. A system of large nets made of braided limbs from trees had been placed in the river to create a fish trap but there were no fish left to be caught in this part of the river. One woman told of eating bark and the gummy sap off a tree. Perhaps she had, but she was still hungry and ate everything that was given her.

One thing puzzled Pro. Many people had died, roughly one out of three, yet there were no corpses to be seen, no sign of funerals, no mourning, and there was no mention of the dead.

"I'm sorry to learn that Goot is dead," Pro said to one Efrin as he handed out food. He hoped to coax some information. The man looked up at him with a blank stare, shrugged his shoulders and walked off. Pro talked to another as he gave him some food. The man grabbed the food and quickly blended in the crowd without responding. Pro never got an answer from anyone and he feared the worst. His stomach began to turn as he looked at the crowd of emaciated phantoms. They milled about holding every crumb of food given them as if it were precious gold. One man dropped some food in the dirt and immediately dropped to his knees and retrieved it, dirt and all.

Finally one woman appeared from the crowd who grabbed Pro's sleeve and wanted to talk. Tears welled up in her eyes as she blurted out, "The bones are over there." She broke down, gasping and sobbing. "They are buried on the other side of the river."

"Over there?" Pro pointed. "Where the willow trees are?" He knew the willow trees very well for he had smuggled his ore boats under the low hanging branches two nights before. "Yes. We couldn't help ourselves," she continued. "We had to eat." She clutched his sleeve tighter. "We were desperate! Don't you understand? We had to eat!" She was pleading now. She dropped to her knees and sobbed, "My daughter and her newborn baby died in childbirth two days ago."

Pro swallowed hard. "Yes." A lump formed in his throat.

"We had to eat them to live."

"Had to eat ... them? The baby?"

"Yes, we ate the dead," the women added quickly. "But only after they died - we NEVER killed anyone and ate them." She was attempting to justify the grisly acts, wiping away the tears on her sleeve. She paused, took a deep breath and thought maybe she had said too much. So she took her food and quickly got lost in the crowd. Pro didn't see her again the rest of the day.

Pro couldn't fathom the notion of eating anyone, let alone your own kin. He felt nauseated and enraged at learning this and his image of the Efrins plunged to the lowest possible depths. Were they worth feeding? he wondered. Were they no better than vultures? They didn't prepare their dead for burial at Stonehenge, and the Efrins didn't ever want to talk about their dead relatives, kinfolk with whom they had worked side by side for long, backbreaking hours in the field; brothers and sisters who supported each other through the agony of unexplained sicknesses, death and now famine; husbands and wives, aunts and uncles that shared the ecstasy of new birth and closeness and interdependence of family.

Pro was furious, and he called his troops together. Stepping on an elevated place on the ground he announced, "Gather all the food together and wrap it in deer skin. We're taking it all back to the fort." He walked over to his men and told them personally, "Pick up the food, we are leaving, now." He walked up to Jep and helped him put food in his bag. Then he walked to Qua and helped her. "Let's go!" he shouted.

Jep was confused. "Why take the food away, now, when they were beginning to make progress?" He did not want to challenge Pro directly but he did not understand. "Pro? The dandelion brew is just beginning to heat up." He lied, for the fire was just starting and the dandelion brew was barely warm. "It's too hot to carry up the hill to the fort. Can we leave it with the Efrins?"

"We're going to leave here and let these animals starve to death. We must leave, now," Pro shouted.

Qua approached Jep. "Why does he want us to leave? These people are not threatening us. What's the matter with Pro?" Jep shook his head and shrugged his shoulders. Pro noticed Qua and Jep talking and Pro yelled, "They eat their dead like vultures. Where are their dead!?" He waved his arms in the air and shouted. "The Efrins have eaten them. Yes, eaten their own family members too. We must leave this place immediately, and get out of here."

He stepped down only to be greeted by a little girl about nine summers old who looked up at him with pathetic eyes and who simply said, "Can I have some food?" She was dressed in a fawn skin skirt that had been cut just for her dainty little figure. Her cheeks were sunken and her skin was pulled over her body so tightly that one could see the outline of bones.

Now Pro was a Stonehenge man, callous and brutalized by the harsh environment, but still he was a human being. He rummaged through his waist pouch for something to give her. He held a generous piece of smoked deer meat his hand, his favorite, and was about to give it to the girl. He decided at the last minute to substitute a dried up piece of unleavened bread. He looked at the young girl.

Her eyes spoke volumes. They were brown, deep set in pools of water. They were sad yet hopeful. With all her misery she managed a faint smile which said "thank you" and "bless you" without saying a word.

Pro bent down to her and held out his hand to her. She placed her hand in his as he asked, "What's your name?"

"Tam."

"Well, Tam, when did you have some food last?"

"Two days ago. Grandma died and we ate her. I have part of my Grandma in me and it will make me be just like her." She smiled proudly. "Grandma made my dress, see? It's my very best one." She did a little curtsy to show all the frills on her dress. "Mommy said that Grandma died so that we could live. She said Grandma wanted it that way, and I love my Grandma." She smiled and continued, "Do you have a Grandma?"

Pro stood silently in a trance. Finally little Tam asked again, "Do you have a grandmother?"

"No - why no, ah, Tammy, my grandmother died long ago. Here, Tammy take this bread." Pro fumbled the piece of old bread and gave it to Tammy. "It isn't much but it is better than nothing."

"Can I save some of this and give it to my mother?"

Pro glanced at the bread and then back at Tammy's eyes. Pro was so affected that he gave her the food he had saved for himself in his knapsack. "Here's some smoked deer meat, Tam. And here's some dandelion brew. It's good for you and it will make you feel better." He patted her on the head, smiled and said, "And, yes, take some to your mother."

Little Tam had said it all very well. It was customary to take the bones of the older generation to a shrine and pray that the children of the present generation will inherit the characteristics of the dead. Eating them is just an extension of that belief, Pro thought. If I were starving I would have done the same thing. "Jep, tell the men to bring the food back. Let's feed them because they need it."

Jep looked at Qua and they shared a quiet smile.

Dun came to Pro in a nervous rage. "I can't find my father. Pro, what have they done with my father?"

"Where have you looked?" He put his arm around her shoulder trying to console her. A terrible thought occurred to Pro. Could Dun's father have been one of those cannibalized?

"I have looked everywhere. I've looked in every hut and under every boat and I can't find him." She broke down, put her head on Pro's shoulder and cried.

"Have you asked anyone about him? Now that they are getting some food, maybe you can talk to them."

She pulled herself together and wiped the tears from her eyes. "Yes! They all seem to avoid me. They don't --" She started to cry again, then caught herself. "They don't want to talk about it."

Pro took Dun to Tam and her playmates. The children hugged them and wouldn't let them go. Pro hoped that Dun would be as touched as he was by little Tam. He thought he must tell Dun what he had found out, and this would be the place. "Dun, I don't know how to tell you this but I'll tell you what I know," he began awkwardly. "Dun, these people, the Efrins, many who used to be here have died. Did you know that?"

"Yes, I knew they had lost a lot of their people," she said without expression.

"Well, the Efrins had to have food so - well, they had to eat their own dead in order to live." He got it out. It wasn't pretty, but then, it wasn't a pretty message no matter how you said it.

Dun stood up and stared at the children momentarily. "You mean you think they ate my father?"

"I don't know. He's missing and he was spitting up blood. That could have weakened him and he could have died."

Dun stood in stunned silence. Her arms hung limp and lifeless by her side. Then she started to walk away. "I'm going back to our fort," she said, fighting back tears. "I can't stand it any more." She walked a few steps, then turned around and shouted, "I hate these people. I hate them." Then she ran towards the Nese hill fort.

Jep was serving dandelion brew to an Efrin when he noticed Dun. He ran to her side and yelled, "Dun! Dun! It's about your father, isn't it?"

She stopped and turned to Jep and nodded, fighting tears.

"I'm so sorry, Dun. Really sorry." He looked at the bowl of brew in his hand and said, "Here, drink this. It's Pro's brew. And you know what he says -- that it's good for anything." She smiled through her tears and drank some. "Well, good. I'm glad you drank that." Jep gave Dun a gentle squeeze with his coarse and weathered hand and they walked to the hill fort together. He stayed with her the rest of the day.

By early afternoon the Efrins had received enough nourishment and water to sustain them and give them hope. They felt assured that more food was available, and they began to look positively towards the future. Pro was pleased with his small group of traders, -- Jep, Qua, Ola, Oma and the others -- for they had worked hard, had never stopped nor complained. They simply considered it their duty to do all they could to help the Efrins. It had been an exceedingly busy and tiring day, but one that Pro was proud of.

CHAPTER 11 GOR'S REQUEST

Several summer solstices passed and gradually the Efrin clan reestablished itself. Many Efrins, however, never completely recovered from their tragedy. Some died, some went blind and some went crazy, while many never functioned as whole human beings again. It was the worst tragedy that the Stonehenge people ever experienced. Other clans nearby suffered from the famine as well, and depended on Pro to provide for them. The Nese clan gradually grew stronger and more dominant in the Salisbury Plain region.

There was no time to dwell on these bitter experiences for there was always work to be done, food to be provided and danger looming in the forest. Calamities were a part of life for the Stonehenge people. Pro had to make repeated trading trips to the south and bargain for more corn, wheat and cassiterite ore. Fortunately the clans near Cornwall had bountiful harvests and had extra grain to trade. They were eager to trade for bronze tools and weapons.

Mott continued to experiment with beeswax and to make more and better bronze tools and weapons. He made large buckets and cauldrons for food preparation, which enabled the clans to boil water and make large amounts of mush and gruel safely. He made smaller bowls for drinking. It was discovered that food tasted better from the bronze bowls than from the leather stitched bowls or from the clay pottery. Moreover, bronze bowls never leaked as the leather bowls often did, and the leather bowls frequently had a faint taste of leather.

Mott's crew improved the smelting process by building an elevated fire place with a safer tripod receptacle holder for the molten bronze. A four- footed receptacle rocked back and forth when placed on uneven ground while the tripod design was very stable. A fire much hotter than that used for cooking was necessary, so charcoal was made from hard oak logs. Two men kept a fire hot with forced air from two goat skin bladders used as bellows. They worked as a team to keep an unbroken blast of air on the coals. One man would force air out, creating hot coals, while the other man would be pulling the skin apart of a second bladder sucking air in. Two other men were kept busy adding fuel to the fire.

In another shop, Mott's men pounded out the cooled metal into thin sheets, then riveted them together and made knives and crude halberds. He turned sheet bronze into a coiled tube with a large bell shape on one end and a crude mouthpiece on the other. This contraption was patterned after the ram's horn.

Several full moons later, when Pro returned from his last trading trip, he was immediately summoned. "Come to your father's hut. Hurry," cried one of the men. "He is very sick."

The family had gathered around Gor who was moaning, crying and thrashing about in pain. His bed of furs and straw had been scattered all over the hut floor. "It's my head, my head," he moaned. "It feels like it is going to burst open." Some of the women quickly moistened his head with sponges made of puffball mushrooms soaked in water. His face was ashen and his clothing was wet with perspiration and he grabbed his head in his hands and ground his teeth in pain.

Pro, accompanied by Mott, stood outside the hut and looked in at the man he had loved and respected all his life. He was speechless; then he noticed something unusual on his father's head. He came inside to get a closer look. The left side of his skull had been shaved clean with a special flint stone razor. In the middle of the shaved area a hole about the size of a kidney bean had been bored through his skull. This was common practice considered necessary to relieve the pressure on the brain caused by evil spirits. It was a brutal task which took four or five men to hold the patient still while the clan doctor punched a hole with a hammer and chisel.

Pro stood shocked in disbelief for he never thought this operation would have to be done to his father. "I see they have punched this hole in Father's head," his voice quivered.

"Yes! We had too," Mott said. "He was in such pain that we had to let the evil spirits out. We had to." Mott shook his head and took a deep breath. "We did it after everything else failed."

"How long has he been like this?"

"It started the day after you left for Cornwall. It wasn't bad at first, but then he got worse. We gave him garlic to draw out the pain and calm him down. It worked for a while, but then we tried barberry tea to gargle to reduce the pain. It worked for a while too."

"He's going to die, isn't he?" Pro interrupted.

Mott simply nodded.

For a moment the pain was less in Gor's head and he became more aware of what was happening around him. "Mott, Pro, come here. I want to say something to you." They gathered close to Gor. "I'm going to journey to the dark side of the moon soon, I know it and I want to be buried here at the fort." His voice grew weak and everyone came close to listen.

"I didn't hear you." Pro bent closer. The Nese clan had a barrow near Stonehenge where every clan chief had been buried for over two thousand years. It was sacrilegious and blasphemous to change that custom.

"I said that when I die I want to be buried at this fort." Gor spoke louder and paused allowing the message to sink in. "Zeff was wrong telling the farmers to plant so early. Zeff was wrong! Anyway, we did more to save the Stonehenge people than Zeff ever did. We saved them because we wanted to feed them." He coughed and blew his nose on his sleeve. "Oh, oh my head -- I want to be buried close to where we did the most good for the starving Efrins and the other clans." He was exhausted and it took all his energy to talk. He reached up and firmly grabbed Pro's arm, looking directly into his son's face. "I want to be buried here so I will," he coughed, "so I will," His voice trailed off and was barely audible. "So I will return to the earth with my people."

He motioned for Mott to bend closer. "Listen carefully. I want my flesh to be cremated at a funeral fire." Pro looked at Mott and both nodded. "Then, I want my bones laid in a crouched position on my left side. I want to face the eastern sunrise so I will know the beginning of each new day. But -- ," he raised his head slightly, "I want my bronze sword at my side." The bronze sword was the first one Mott had made with a beeswax mold and Gor treasured it.

Pro looked at Mott and they nodded again. This was the usual way for burial.

Gor grasped Pro's arm tighter. "I want a chambered tomb. I want a burial chamber with stone slab walls and a massive slab on top. Make the entrance chamber the same way and cover it with a mound of dirt this high." He motioned from his shoulders to his feet. "But don't cover the entrance with dirt. I want a heavy stone at the door to keep animals and people away from my bones." Pro knew the barrow of which Gor spoke.

Gor's hand dropped lifeless on his straw pillow and he took a deep breath and in a husky voice said, "That's what I want. Then I can join your mother." And so he died.

Silence fell on Pro like a leaden blanket, suffocating his very soul. "Join Mother?" Pro looked at Mott. "Join Mother, what does he mean by that? Is Mother dead too!?"

"Yes, Pro," Mott mumbled. "Mother died from a snake bite six days after you left. She is buried in the barrow that Dad just talked about." Pro felt like he had been kicked in the stomach and was gasping for air. He was too much of a man to cry, and too human not to.

It was one full moon after Gor's cremation and burial when three unexpected guests arrived at the fort. They marched into the center of the court yard in stern military fashion, summoned the guard and announced, "We want Pro, son of Gor of the Nese clan. Bring him to us." The guard was puzzled. They weren't clan chieftains, for they carried only a walking shaft and small swords for protection. They weren't farmers, for they did not wear clothing made of furs. Nor were they a band of renegade hunters for they did not carry bows and arrows. They didn't even have dogs for protection in the night. They were dressed in black wool capes which hung loosely to their ankles. It was the best kind of wool, skillfully crafted by an excellent weaver. They carried little other clothing or provisions in their backpacks. "Would you like to sit under the tree and rest while I fetch Pro?" asked the nervous guard.

"No, we will stay here." They stood studying the fort and all the people they could see.

"Would you like some food or water? You must have been traveling a long way." The guard knew that they were not local folk, for he knew everyone within five miles of the fort.

"Not till we see Pro," said the leader. His face was stern and expressionless. By now most work activity had stopped in the fort and everyone stood around with mouths gaping open staring at the strangers.

"Yes, I'll, I'll find Pro." The guard hurried off.

Pro was in the smelting room with Mott preparing for the next trading trip. "We will load two boats with the pottery the Efrins have made. It trades well with the people at Cornwall," he proposed.

"And another two boats with wool from the Host clan to the north," added Mott. Pro nodded agreement. All the nearby clans were deeply in debt to the Nese clan for providing them food, and trading their wares was the only way they could repay.

"We will fill the rest of the boats with bronze ware and food for the trip. I want to save some space for several of those horns you made." They both laughed. "It's a toy, I know, but all the chiefs I trade with like them. I play a few toots and show them how it works. Then they try it and we trade--like this." He played a few raucous noises and they both bent over in laughter.

"It sounds like an ox farting," said Mott. He slapped his knee and they laughed some more.

The guard rushed to the hut. "Pro, there are three strange men standing in the courtyard who insist on seeing you."

The guard was nervous and breathless, and Pro sensed his urgency. He put the horn down and looked at Mott who merely shrugged his shoulders. Then he walked to the hut entrance. Pro separated the hanging skin door just enough to see out and took a long studied look at the three men. "I don't know who they are. Do you, Mott?"

Mott rubbed his chin. "They are a queer looking group, aren't they? I've never seen them before."

"They demand to see you right away," the guard emphasized.

"Well, tell them that they are interfering with my horn playing. This is important work." Pro and Mott exchanged glances and snickered. They both went to meet the strangers.

The men were still standing around rather impatiently. "We came for Pro, son of Gor of the Nese clan," one said. There were no introductions, no greeting, just commands.

Pro did not answer at first. He didn't like the haughty attitude of the men and could have taken them prisoner with the wave of a hand. Slowly he walked among the three, examining them from head to toe. He motioned to Mott, who was holding a shiny bronze sword about three feet long. "This is Mott, my brother," said Pro. "Show them the sword you have made, Mott."

Mott stood at attention and held the sword directly in front of him with the point extended to the ground. Then he thrust the sword into a nearby tree. He swung the sword around and passed it across their wool capes, causing them to back away for safety. He lunged the blade between their feet causing them to jump quickly, and ended as he had started, snapping to attention and holding the sword in front of him. "He makes bronze swords. This sword is a battle sword and it has a bloodstain on the blade." Pro pointed to a spot on the sword which actually was a berry stain. "It is an excellent weapon." The meaning was clear, and the three strangers knew they were guests at Pro's bidding.

"Now, what do you want from Pro?" Mott asked.

"Zeff has instructed us to bring Pro to Stonehenge."

"Zeff? Stonehenge?" said Mott. This explained their arrogant manner and made a bit more sense out of their visit. Only the chief priest at Stonehenge could summon people. "Why does he want to see Pro?"

"He has instructed us to bring him to Stonehenge. That's all I know."

Pro stepped forward, extended his hand and said, "Well, I'm Pro. I'm Zeff's cousin, you know. We have the same grandfather. I'd like to see him, too."

The leader was startled. He didn't know that Pro and Zeff were related. The formality had stopped and there was some cordial exchange. "Well, let me explain. I'm Yam, Zeff's chief assistant."

Now Pro noticed the white, cream -colored scar on Yam's left cheek. "I know you, Yam. We met at Stonehenge when Zeff became chief priest. Do you remember?"

"Yes, yes. You were at Stonehenge with your wife and family. Yes, I remember now."

They exchanged hand clasps at the wrist and Pro said, "You must join us for dinner, and then after a good night's sleep we will make our journey to Stonehenge."

CHAPTER 12 THE ENCOUNTER WITH ZEFF

It was late in the afternoon of the next day when Yam and Pro reached the Stonehenge shrine. The bronze sunset framed each stone with a golden edge as if it were individually blessing each stone. Their elongated shadows stretched out over the grounds, making Stonehenge appear bigger and more impressive than Pro had ever remembered. Pro had never seen Stonehenge at this time of day. He was moved by the silent grandeur and stopped briefly to absorb the magic of the moment.

Pro was taken to the shelter where the clay tablets were stored. "Pro, how are you?" Zeff greeted Pro with a broad smile. His goatee was meticulously combed and waxed with deer fat. He had sagging rolls of fat in his cheeks and he was a bit rotund around the middle. Pro was dismayed and disappointed, for fat men were rare in the world of Stonehenge. A fat person was immediately noticed and considered gluttonous and a parasite by his hard-working peers. Furthermore, a fat person was held in contempt and distrust by starving people. Pro, on the other hand, was wiry and sinewy, toughened by the elements.

Zeff was lounging in a comfortable chair behind his table of clay tablets of Stonehenge. The seat was made soft with layers of heavy furs. Pro sat on a bench directly across from him. On a table between them were two clay tablets which were the replica of the stones of Stonehenge. "How good to see you." He rocked back and forth and finally freed himself from his chair, stood and greeted Pro with a slight bow. "It has been a long time since we have seen each other."

"Yes, Zeff, it has been nearly two summer solstices since Qua, the twins and I were here, and you showed us the mysteries of Stonehenge. I still remember everything."

"I remember your visit too. I gave you a private tour of the shrine." He spread his hands out, palms upward, as if he were offering a prayer. "Let us drink a toast." He poured Pro a cup of mead from a polished bronze vase and they toasted. "And Qua, Oma and Ola, are they in good health?"

"Yes, the twins will soon be of age and Ola will be given the rite of adulthood. And Qua has been helping on our trading trips at Cornwall. I couldn't trade without her. She lost her baby but is healthy again." They toasted in mead, which was unbearably sweet by Pro's palate but was Zeff's favorite drink.

"So Ola has grown up. Soon he will come to Stonehenge for training in the priesthood." Zeff said as he took a sip of mead. He glanced over his cup and added, "We talked briefly about that when you were here last. Do you remember? -- I'm looking foreword to training him for this responsible position."

Pro was pensive remembering how the twins reacted to going to Stonehenge when they were camped at the river Avon. They did not want to leave the clan and they did not want to be separated. Neither Qua nor Pro had mentioned the subject since then. "Yes, they are growing up, and Oma, of course, is becoming a young women. Is there a place for her in the priesthood? Also, they are close twins, very close. It would be difficult to separate them."

"Well, we don't have to settle that today. It's been too long since we have seen each other. My, my. .. You know, I miss the old days when we were boys and played together. Don't you?"

"Yes, It seems a long time ago,"

Pro nodded. The two had been inseparable when they were young. They played together in the fields and orchards and they worked together gathering nuts and mushrooms. It was always understood, however, that Zeff was to become chief priest of Stonehenge and Pro would enter the family trade business. Not only had they shared childhood pleasures together, but they shared a particular secret. Zeff never went swimming with the rest of the boys. This was because Zeff was monorchid, that is, he had only one testicle. If he swam in the nude with the other boys they would tease him and embarrass him unmercifully. Pro knew his secret and never told anyone. Because of this, a bond of trust and friendship had developed between the two boys that extended into adulthood. It is also true that Zeff never took a mate.

"Some of the things we did. Wow! Do you remember the fire we made in the hay hut? We almost burned all the hay stored there for winter," Zeff said.

"I remember that. We were trying to make fire by striking flint sparks into the hay and -- we succeeded."

"I'll say we succeeded." Zeff laughed.

"Then your dad came and smothered the fire with his cape and dragged us out of the hut."

"We are lucky to be alive, you and I. Some of the things we did as boys." Zeff motioned to Yam, who was standing outside the shelter beyond hearing distance but near enough to see. "Bring us some light. It's getting dark." Zeff took a long drink of his mead, then began. "I was sorry to hear about your father's death."

"Yes, Father died after the operation to let the evil spirits out of his head."

"He was cremated?"

"Yes, his bones are in a barrow." There was a heavy silence as Zeff walked back to his seat fingering his pointed beard. Pro wondered why Zeff didn't ask about his mother, who had died also, and Mott and the rest of the family. He also wondered why Zeff wanted him here. It was not like Zeff to commandeer him and then reminisce about their youth. Pro knew Zeff was after more. Finally Pro said, "Their death was a big loss, but Mott and I have adjusted fairly well."

Zeff leaned forward and looked across the table of clay figures. "And buried at your hill fort, wasn't he?"

Pro took a long time sipping his mead before answering. So this is why I've been brought here, he thought. Zeff is upset because Father is not buried in the family barrow near Stonehenge. Pro looked at the man across from him who was rocking back and forth with his hands folded in front. Finally Pro said, "This mead is good." Pro held up the beaker in a toasting manner. "This comes from the best honey made from gallery and soured blossoms," Pro added. He was purposely evasive. Pro took another sip. "The Jots clan gives this mead to you every spring as an offering, I believe, and it's the best mead you can get. I know; I trade bronze with them." He took a final sip and filled his beaker again.

Finally he answered Zeff's question. "Yes, Father wanted to be buried at the fort, and Mott and I had a barrow made and buried him there. But let me ask you a question. Why was I brought here like a prisoner? We are related and we can talk as cousins should."

"Well, it's not too late. You say you have the bones?" Pro nodded, deciding not to give Zeff the satisfaction of a verbal answer.

Zeff sat back in his log chair. "We can have his bones brought here to your family barrow at Stonehenge. I personally will perform the high sacred burial rite. I would be honored to do this, truly honored."

Pro took another slow sip of mead and collected his thoughts. "That would be good of you, Zeff." He paused. "We will certainly talk it over the next time I'm with Mott and the elders of the Nese clan. I know it's important for you to have all the clan chieftains buried in their ancestral barrows here at Stonehenge."

"Important? It's absolutely necessary for him to be buried here. At Stonehenge we are in such immediacy with the life-giving sun and harvest moon. You must have his bones moved now, before the gods become angry with you."

"Gods? Angry? Father wanted to be buried at the hill fort. It was a dying man's last wish. He wanted his bones to stay at the fort too. The spirit of my dead father would haunt me if I moved the bones. The spirit would never stop haunting me." Pro placed his cup on the table with a loud thud and pushed it away towards Zeff. "He would haunt me during daylight and even worse during the blackness of night. I would never be free."

Zeff's face turned gray and he took a slow, deliberate sip of mead. Finally he said, "Men say strange things before they die. They can become possessed with the evil spirits from the dark side of the moon. Are you sure he actually knew what he said? He did have a hole punched in his head, which probably left him in a dazed state." Zeff shrugged his shoulders. "Probably his mind was possessed by the dark side of the moon and he was not himself at all."

Pro knew that his father knew exactly what he was doing and saying. "Well, I will consult with Mott and the rest of the clan. It is not a decision I can make alone."

Zeff rose from his chair and walked around the clay tablets on the table. "Pro, you must bury him here at Stonehenge."

Pro looked straight at Zeff. "And the spirits of a dead man, Zeff, what about them? Wouldn't those spirits haunt you, too? You are the chief priest, and you would be responsible because you insisted that a dead man be buried here against his last wish. My father would haunt both of us until we die and after."

This revelation came down hard on Zeff, and he drank his mead in one gulp, then poured himself more. He offered mead to Pro, who politely refused. Then Zeff leaned forward and confidentially revealed, "No clan chieftains have been buried at Stonehenge since the famine, Pro. I don't know what is wrong. Where are the Efrim chiefs and the chiefs of the other clans that have died? None of them have been buried in their clan barrows. I thought if you could have your father buried here, the rest would follow and we would be in favor with the gods again."

Pro thought, Zeff knows nothing about the terrible famine. The burned scar on his cheek began to tingle and Pro rubbed it. Must I be the one to tell him this news?

"I think the gods will be angry with me," Zeff continued. "It is my responsibility to have the dead chieftains buried here at Stonehenge. You know that over 120 families have their burial barrows within a day's walking distance of Stonehenge. Did you know that, Pro?"

Pro said, "I knew there were a great many barrows here, yes." He nodded.

"Clans have been buried here for thousands of summer solstices." Zeff paused. "The clan families have always wanted to be buried here. They brought their dead here. No priest EVER had to ask the clan to bury the dead here." He was practically shouting now. "I don't know what went wrong. Why do they do this to me?" His expression was downcast. "Do they want us to fall into disfavor with the gods?" Zeff became agitated, nervously fingering his beard, and he wiped perspiration from his forehead.

"I don't think that's true, Zeff." Pro tried to console him. "I don't know - let me think about it?" Pro knew that Zeff was easily angered, and he felt that Zeff was close to losing control. He decided to change the subject.

"When we were here before, you were working on measuring time. You observed that the summer solstice occurred every 364 sun rises or was it 365 sun rises? You thought it was a dependable measure of time. Am I right?"

"Yes, but the summer solstice is not that regular." Zeff had cooled down some, but the problem with the clan chiefs not being buried at Stonehenge was just below the surface of his thinking. "The full moon occurs every 29 or 30 days, and it is impossible to figure how many full moons there are in 364 days. It doesn't make sense."

Pro reached for his mead, raised his cup and said, "Zeff, there is a time to break the soil from winter's bondage, a time to plant the seeds, a time to work the crops, a time to harvest the bounty and a time for winter sleep. I think your plan of measuring time is clearly a mark of achievement and you should continue to study it."

"Except it doesn't work. Three solstices ago I told the farmers to plant earlier, and they did as I commanded, and I understand some of their crops were frozen and destroyed."

Pro pondered, Is that all he knows about the starvation and death? Pro realized he must fish for more information to determine exactly how much Zeff really knew.

"What about the farmers?" Pro asked.

"Well, some of them died. I don't want to talk about it now. It wasn't all my fault, you know. It was an unusually cold spring that year. It would have been a bad year even if I hadn't told the farmers to plant early. It rained and snowed all spring and ruined the planting time. It wasn't all my fault."

"That's true," conceded Pro. "It was a bad year. The goddess of fertility did not allow spring to begin till very late. It wasn't all your fault."

"Why aren't the Efrin chieftains buried here? Where is the Jost chieftain buried? The Gotts, the Itta, and the Hosts? I know the chiefs of these clans have died. Why aren't they buried in their clan barrows here at Stonehenge?"

"Because they are buried elsewhere," Pro said. "They were all hurt badly when the fertility goddess did not allow the plants to grow, and they are buried where they died. The families didn't have the strength to bury their dead chiefs in the clan barrows."

"Didn't have the strength? I don't understand."

"The famine was really bad for some clans. Bad like the Wan clan. Remember many summer solstices ago when so many of the Wan families were killed by wind, storm and flooding?"

"The Wan clan? Everyone died there. You don't mean everyone died from the famine?"

"No, but a lot of people died, and there was great suffering, and no one really knows where some of the people are buried."

"We can find the bones and bring them here, can't we?" persisted Zeff.

"Maybe."

"Maybe?"

"The Efrin took their bones to the sunrise side of the river and left them there. They were so hungry that they ate everything. Everything." Pro paused and looked at Zeff hoping to see some emotional reaction, some slight facial scowl or frown that would indicate that he was aware of the cannibalism.

Zeff's face remained unflappable. "Well, go on, Pro, what happened next?"

"When the Efrins died, they could not help themselves, and they ate their own dead. We could find their bones from the pile on the sunrise side of the river and bring them here."

Zeff's eyes became glossy, and he shook his head in disbelief. "Ate their own dead? Did you say they ate their dead?" His voice was barely audible. "And they didn't bury them, just piled the bones! You mean there were no cremations, no funeral ritual, no driving the spirits of dead away, no preparation of the barrows for the dead? It is no wonder that the gods are angry with us!"

"The Efrins, they walked around like ghosts, not able to do anything. It was terrible. They were so hungry they even ate their fish bait and seed corn. They had to eat their guard dogs too." Pro stood up and paced in front of the table. "They even let their fires go out. They were desperate, Zeff, simply desperate. They were dying. I, I thought you knew!"

Zeff continued to shake his head in disbelief. There was a long silence as Zeff pondered, then he clutched Pro's arm with a rigid grip. "The others, what about the other clans? What happened to them? Did they eat their dead too?"

"What others?"

"The Hosts and the Ittas and the others. What happened to them?"

"A lot of them died too. It was very bad for the Stonehenge clans."

"Did they eat their dead?"

"I don't know. I can't be sure. I heard they did."

Zeff rose from his chair and yelled, "You don't know? What do you mean, you don't know? You must know. Someone must know. No one wants to tell me the truth." He pointed his finger in Pro's face. "Not even you, Pro, my cousin, my childhood friend. No one wants to tell me the truth. Am I so weak that I cannot stand to hear the truth?"

"Well, you know the truth now, Zeff. I don't know why you haven't been told. I'm, I'm sorry that I have to be the one to tell you this. Someone else should have told you long ago."

"Starving, a famine, that's why they haven't sent any food to the Stonehenge priests." Zeff was pacing back and forth, waving his hands in the air. "We've got to have food and clothing here at the Stonehenge. We are not farmers, we're priests! The farmers have always brought us food, gifts and clothing." Beads of sweat formed on his forehead and he wiped his brow with his sleeve. "Pro, we are running low on food. We have never been so low on food before!"

He wiped the sweat from his forehead with his hand. Then he stopped in his tracks and pointed to the bowl of mead on the table. "Look at that. Look at those black worms crawling out of the mead bowl." He looked at Pro and said, "Can't you see them? Look!" He shook his finger at the bowl. "Can't you see them? Pro, tell me you can see them too!" He was almost pleading.

Pro stopped and stared. The bowl was in the shadows and he barely saw it. "Why yes, I see. I see the bowl, but I don'–--."

Just then Yam arrived. "Here is a lamp light, Zeff."

Zeff motioned for Yam to set the lamp down. He placed the light directly in front of the bowl of mead. The polished bronze bowl sparkled with dazzling miniature diamond like flashes of light. Clearly there were no black worms. Yam held the skin door open as he left and a cold blast of air flickered the flame, causing grotesque demon-like shadows on the wall of the shelter. "Is there anything else?" Yam asked.

Zeff ignored Yam. "They hate me. The clans hate me. But I didn't cause the fertility goddess to be late." He rose from his seat and pointed at Pro. "It was a cold spring, you understand. There would have been a famine anyway. But they hate me for it. The gods are getting impatient with me. The gods hate me too."

Pro starred at the cup again. It was an ordinary bronze cup, nothing special. Then he studied Zeff and concluded that something was definitely wrong. The wick on the lamp sputtered, and light was uneven. A black trace of smoke rose from the light which smelled like rancid fat.

"Well, we must do something about the Efrins and all the other clans," Zeff continued, regaining some composure. "I want you to bring the bones of the chiefs here so we can give them the proper funeral rite and bury them in the barrows. First bring your father's bones here, and we will bury him. Then the others will follow." He walked away from the shelter and out into the night, apparently oblivious to a cold drizzle which settled on his face. Zeff looked in the direction of the great Stonehenge arches but was denied a view. It had been cut off by a cloud of mist. Then Zeff cried out, "The gods are angry!" He stopped and shouted back at Pro. "The gods are angry with me." He pointed at Pro. "You talk about your father's dead spirits haunting you." Then he pointed at himself. "There are hundreds of dead spirits haunting me. Hundreds. Everyone hates me. The clans hate me." He came back inside dripping wet from the rain.

Pro shook his head. "No, they don't hate you. They wonder why you didn't come and feed them when they were hungry. A starving man needs only one thing -- food!" Pro answered in the most even controlled voice he could muster. "If it hadn't been for my father and our clan, they all would have starved. Dead! We brought them food." Pro slumped back in his chair. He was sweating profusely, for he didn't believe what he was hearing. Zeff, the most promising, enlightened priest he had known, was coming apart. "They don't hate you, Zeff. They just don't understand you."

"They do hate me. Otherwise they would bring their dead here and they would bring food. They do hate me!" His face was flushed red. "There they go again. See them?" Zeff pointed to the table. "Can't you see them, Pro?" Zeff was shouting. "There by the bowl. Can't you see them? The black worms are crawling out of the bowl. The worms are crawling. The weeerms."- Zeff's eyes became crossed and he went limp and lifeless. With one broad sweep of his arm Zeff wiped everything off the table and smashed it to the floor. The clay tablets of Stonehenge were cracked and distorted. Then he slumped down on the table and passed out, spilling his mead on himself.

Early the next morning, before Zeff and the other priests had awakened, Pro quietly gathered his clothing in a knapsack and left Stonehenge. He gave Yam a message the night before that he would bring the bones of the chiefs back to Stonehenge for burial. "Zeff has had too much mead. When he wakes up, tell him I have a 'plan' that I know will work."

As he prepared to walk from his quarters, he was interrupted. Two young girls, not much older than Oma, came running into his quarters. They grabbed Pro by his sleeve and pleaded, "Take us with you. Can you take us with you?"

"Shh, don't awake anyone." Pro motioned. "What's wrong? Why are you here in my quarters?"

"It's Zeff. He's so bad to us. He beats us when he can't perform."

"Yes, and it is he who can't perform. We're scared. Really scared he might sacrifice us to the gods."

Pro put his knapsack down and sat on the edge of his bunk. He pondered what to do next. "He can't perform and then he blames you?"

"Yes, it's true, but no one believes us. He wants to have a mate and he wants to have children, but he can't. He can't." She commenced uncontrolled sobbing.

"Don't tell anyone we were here. If this ever gets out Zeff will sacrifice us to the gods, I'm so scared," pleaded the second girl.

Pro held the two girls gently by the arm, smiled as pleasantly as he could. "I believe you, and I understand this about Zeff."

The girls were still afraid, but hopeful. "Zeff would kill us if he knew we were here."

"I'll see what I can do. I can't do anything now, for I must go, but I'll do something as soon as I can. Now, you better leave." Pro picked up his knapsack and left.

As he walked away from Stonehenge, he turned and took a long last look back. The monument had become smaller when viewed from a distance, and in the purer light of the morning sunshine it seemed diminished in size and significance. Zeff's drunken episode and the desperate girls had left Pro puzzled. He felt that something was lacking in the great Stonehenge religion. There was a void, an absence of compassion for the needs of others. Something that his father had realized was necessary and had lived by.

He thought of little Tam, the starving young Efrin girl whose life he had saved. She said her thanks with her eyes. The brown dreamy eyes of this innocent young girl remained fixed in his memory as he left Stonehenge and Zeff behind. Somehow Tammy and all she represented was more important to Pro than all the grand tradition of Stonehenge.

CHAPTER 13 AVEBURY

Pro did not travel toward the sunrise to his clan at the hill fort. At the last minute, he decided to walk south along the Icknied Way to Avebury shrine to see Wam, the chief priest. Pro didn't know how Zeff would feel when he sobered up. Would he have him followed by his priests and commandeered again or worse? If so, Pro would be at the Avebury shrine and not at the clan fort and no one would know where he was, not even his brother, Mott.

Pro was also distressed and worried about Zeff. Was Zeff sick in the head, struck by the moon, or was he really affected by the spirits of the dead? He remembered how some of the Efrins had acted when they were starving from the famine, how they had walked around in a daze, talking to themselves, and would scream hideous cries for no reason at all, usually in the middle of the night. Some claimed that they were being chased by spiders and terrorized by snakes. Did Zeff have the same sickness as the Efrins, even though he was isolated from the famine? Maybe Zeff was right. Maybe the gods were angry and maybe they were punishing the Stonehenge people. Maybe he had done wrong by not having his father's bones buried at Stonehenge. He wanted desperately to seek the advice of Wam, an old friend of the family.

He traveled a day's journey along the River Kennet and entered Avebury from the south, where he experienced the total spiritual effect of the great shrine. He ran his hand over the smooth polished surface of several of the stone megaliths in the inner circle. He felt a bond, a union with the earth goddess, and a calm came over him. Then he felt the rough outside surface of the stone and thought to himself, this is the stone as nature gives it. This is the gift of life we get from God. Life, in the rough, which is surrounded with the dangers and uncertainties.

He scratched his hand on the ragged surface of the stone and it began to bleed. He did not flinch or bandage it and the blood streaked down his wrist to his elbow. This was symbolic of life's uncertainties and his stoic response was what God had wanted. He felt blessed that God had tested him and he had not flinched.

Again he touched the smooth, polished inside surface of the same stone and thought, this is what man can do with what nature has given. He thought of the great Stonehenge shrine built with sarsen stones, fashioned from raw stones into rectangular megaliths and placed in a tight circle around the horse shoe arches. The grandeur was breathtaking.

The silence of Pro's concentration was broken by Wam's greeting. "Pro," he shouted from a distance and ran to greet him. "Pro, welcome to Avebury." They greeted each other with a slight bow and exchanged the usual polite inquiries about their families and friends. Wam invited Pro to his hut where they sat on comfortable sheepskin seats and talked. Wam finally asked, "And what brings you to Avebury?"

Pro began, hesitantly at first. He told Wam how Zeff and he were trusted friends and confidants from their youth, how they enjoyed reminiscing about their childhood together. He mentioned Zeff's becoming fat and how Zeff enjoyed his mead. They laughed together. "It's easy to become fat when you are a priest because you don't work in the fields," Wam said.

Finally Pro related the whole story. He told about Zeff's attempts to develop a calendar and how Zeff had told the farmers to plant too early in the spring. He told about the famine and the resulting starvation and hardship as a result of the famine. He told of the cannibalism, little Tam and all the unpleasant details.

"The crops have not been very good since the famine, either," Pro added.

"I know, I have heard," said Wam. "It's been wet and foggy here too." Wam was Zeff's senior, and had always felt that he should have been the chief priest at Stonehenge. While Avebury was larger and older, nothing could compare with the greatness and prestige of Stonehenge.

"Some farmers have packed up their families and gone to the north where we hear the weather is better," Pro emphasized. "They have to eat! They have to go where there is food!"

"I know. The farmers have been giving less and less food and clothing to our priests." Wam's face became stern and his forehead creased with thought. "It's a serious problem. The fertility god has –" He stopped short and gulped hard and continued, "The fertility god has to be appeased, restored back to her original position so that we can have the good crops we used to have. But more about Zeff."

Pro spoke of Zeff's anger about the dead not being buried near Stonehenge. He was careful about what he said so the implication would be that Zeff was working hard and was under great stress. Then he told of the black worms that didn't exist in the mead jug and of Zeff passing out over the clay drawings of Stonehenge. "So I got up early this morning and left without saying goodbye. I intended to go back to my clan because I have to make a trading trip to Cornwall, but I decided to come here and talk this over with you."

"Well, I'm glad you did." Wam had a gracious smile and a gentle twinkle in his eyes. He was of Pro's father's generation, and his advice was what Pro wanted. "What do you intend to do now?"

"I'm not sure what I'll do. In fact, I don't know what I can do. I told Yam I had a plan, but it isn't definite. I thought I would ask all the clans affected by the famine to find the bones of their chieftains and prepare them for burial at their clan barrow near Stonehenge. We could have a grand meeting at our hill fort and bring the bones to Stonehenge in a group. Like a pilgrimage. I believe I could do that because I trade bronze with them all the time and, well, I have helped them through the famine. I think I can do this."

Then Pro stopped. He became pensive and silent. His thoughts drifted away and he wondered why Zeff couldn't do the same thing. Zeff could go to the clans himself and arrange to have the bones buried at Stonehenge. He could explain how the gods could become angry better than Pro could. Then it occurred to him that maybe Zeff was so distant from the clans, so removed from their needs, that he couldn't communicate anymore. He questioned how the emaciated clansmen who had never completely recovered from the famine would respond to their corpulent chief priest. How sad, he thought. What a tragedy to be so removed from the needs of the clan.

"Go on, Pro." Wam broke the silence.

"Oh, yes, of course. I think I could do it if the clans knew how urgent it is to be buried at Stonehenge."

"The bones, you say they are all mixed in a pile somewhere?"

"Yes. Each of the four clans just piled the bones as far away from their huts as possible. I don't know how we could find the chief's bones from the rest."

"Well, they must be separated. If you are going to bury the chieftain then you must bury his bones only."

"Is that true?"

"Why, yes. I mean, if you bury a chieftain and have someone else's bones in the barrow you will have great trouble." Wam's face became stern again. "You will have the dead spirits of the chiefs haunting you the rest of your life."

This was something that Pro hadn't considered. "Do you mean me, too?"

"I mean everyone. The dead spirits will not rest, and they would haunt their children and their children's children that offered the wrong bones, and they would haunt the priest that buried them. And yes, you are their leader. The spirits of the dead are the most forceful spirits there are. You know that, don't you?"

"Yes, I knew that the spirits of the dead are strong, but, these people... They were starving... and many of them died. They didn't know..."

"They didn't know? They didn't obey their priests." Wam jumped off his seat and shouted. "The spirits of the mistreated dead will haunt everyone, everyone, and that's all there is to it. Let me tell you something, Pro. The dead spirit of your father is working right now."

"What do you mean?"

"I knew your father very well and he was a good man." Wam leaned over, put his hand on Pro's shoulder and smiled. "His spirit is in you. When you talk, you sound like your father. Your father used to rub his chin when he was thinking and you, well, you rub that little scar on your face. You ask a lot of questions just like your father." A slight smile appeared on Wam's face. "And you act like your father, too. Your mannerisms are the same. I was watching you when you scratched your hand on the rough stone pillar and it bled. Then you bravely ignored it, just like your father would do. So you see, the spirits of the dead are with us in every action we do."

"I guess Zeff is right. They must have a proper burial. We can't allow the bones to be piled up in some unmarked place for vultures and varmints to eat. Surely the dead spirits will rise from those piles and haunt us." Pro stammered and coughed.

"Pro? What are you trying to say?"

"Like they have with Zeff."

"Pro, you think the dead spirits are haunting Zeff now?"

"I don't know. I just don't know." Pro paused for a moment. "Maybe the dead spirits are causing Zeff to see the worms in his mead bowl."

"I don't know about that. I just can't say." There was no twinkling in Wam's eyes now. His merriment and playful nature was gone, driven off by the thought of the unburied dead. He stood up and pointed down at Pro. "First, you must sort through the bones to find the ones of the chieftains and prepare for proper burials!" Wam paced about his hut. "Then you must bury the dead on the feast of the major standstill of the moon rise in the north. That is the closest celestial religious day and a fitting one. It happens every 112 summer solstices."

"Every 112 summer solstices? How do you know these things?"

"We know," Wam said. "It is our business to know."

Pro had sought Wam's advice and had gotten it, but Wam wasn't finished yet.

"You must get the bones sorted, and we must bury them on this moon rise. We can't wait till the next summer solstice." Wam hit his fist against the palm of his hand to emphasize the point.

"Why this particular moon rise? Why not wait until the summer solstice?" Pro knew that the summer solstice was a major feast day, more significant than the northern moon rise.

"Because something horrible might happen if we wait until the summer solstice. On or near the summer solstice, the moon will move in front of the sun and smother it. Black it out."

"Black out the sun? " Pro was practically shouting. "What do you mean smother it? How long will the moon stay in front of the sun?"

"Don't get excited. It will last as long as it takes the sun to rise. How long does it take from the time you first see the sun come up until the full ball appears? That's how long the sun will be darkened. Nothing will change. Zeff will tell everybody about it and everyone will know exactly what will happen. No one need be afraid."

"Why can't the bones be buried at the time the sun is blackened out?"

"The farmers will take it as a bad omen. They will think that the dead spirits are causing the blackness of the sun. And, of course, that is not the way it is at all!"

Pro could not remember if he had ever seen an eclipse of the sun. He remembered seeing a partial eclipse of the moon when he was a young boy and how scared he was. His uncle was chief priest at Stonehenge then, and he explained what was happening over and over again so the adults were not afraid. Surely Zeff would make a proclamation and explain the eclipse of the sun to all the people.

"Now, Pro, we must act quickly. Tomorrow I will travel to Stonehenge and tell Zeff of our visit. I'll confirm that you will talk to the clans and will have the bones ready for burial at the major standstill of the moon rise in the northern sky. He will be glad to hear that, and I think he will be eager to perform a mass burial at that time."

Pro nodded.

"I must go and see if Zeff really is affected by the moon or distraught by the dead buried on the river bank!" He paused, shook his head in disbelief. "Or, if the fertility god is really angry with us, and trying to punish us."

Pro said nothing and nodded again.

"But allow me two days to see Zeff before you go back to your fort. I'm an old man, you know, and I must walk slowly to Stonehenge. You can stay here and sleep with one of my slaves. Maybe with Shana. She is a real beauty and you'll like her."

Pro had traveled long and was weary, and a brief rest in a warm bed with one of Wam's women before returning to the fort would be welcome. Wam clapped his hands and made a motion to his servant. Soon, four young, shapely girls appeared. "Pro will be here for two days. I want you to entertain him as you would entertain me." The girls bowed gracefully. One of the girls moved to the back of the hut and commenced playing a zither-like instrument. The others danced a slow, rhythmic, provocative dance around the two men.

CHAPTER 14 WAM LEARNS ABOUT ZEFF

Wam found Zeff sitting in his hut bent over his clay tablets of Stonehenge. Zeff had a leather string tied to two wooden sticks. One stick he placed in the center of his tablet and the other was stretched to the end of the string where he had inscribed a perfect circle in the moist clay. At the edge of the circle he fashioned a bit of clay into an embankment. "I don't know how this happened," Zeff said, "but I found the clay tablets spread all over the floor, broken. It is just another of the many strange things that have been happening lately."

Wam talked while Zeff worked. He told of Pro's visit and how he reinforced the necessity to have the bones buried at Stonehenge. Zeff nodded agreement and said nothing. Wam said that Pro would bring the bones to Stonehenge. "We've got to do this before we anger the gods," he said.

"Anger the gods? I believe that they are already angry." Zeff spoke in a controlled tone.

"The sooner we bury the dead chieftains the better it will be."

"Yes, of course."

"I suggested that we bury all the chieftains at the feast of the major standstill of the moon rise in the north. That is less than a full moon away."

"That's fine." Zeff was listless, passive, completely in agreement with Wam.

"Of course, I can help you with the holy ceremony if you wish. It will be a burial of five chieftains, and we will have to open five barrows for burial. We will have to perform the ceremony at each barrow, and we will have to complete the task all on the day of the moon rise, won't we?"

"Yes, that's right." Zeff said nothing else.

After a long, awkward pause Wam shifted in his seat and added, "It will be a very busy day, and we will have to start at sunrise and work till sunset."

Zeff simply nodded.

Wam continued, "Can your priests have everything prepared at each of the burial barrows so you and I can conduct the service and move on from one to the other?"

"Yes." Zeff's answers were so unenthusiastic that Wam wondered if Zeff was aware of what he was talking about.

"If we do this as planned, then the gods won't be angry with us."

"Won't be angry? What do you mean 'won't be angry'? They are already angry! How could you think that the gods are not angry?" Zeff was almost combative in his response.

"Well, I --I just--."

Zeff was ignited. He condemned the clans for not donating food and clothing. He ridiculed the clans for not presenting their chiefs for burial voluntarily. He complained about the bad weather and how it had prevented sighting the sacred seasonal celestial observation. "I want the bones. I want the long bones and the skulls of every chieftain here for burial." He stood up and pointed his finger at Stonehenge. "We will clean out the center of the long bones and make whistles and flutes. The noise will scare away the dead spirits. The skulls are cages and must be crushed to release the evil spirits so they will be pure and freed. This is the only way!" He was pacing back and forth. "Death is but one step in the fertility ring. It is a ring of death, the dark world journey and rebirth, adulthood and death again. Earth and man passes from spring, to summer, to winter and back again. It is the way of our ring culture. We must not break that ring! We must bury the dead freed from evil spirits."

Wam could not agree more, for Zeff's theology was perfect. Indeed death was but one part of the fertility cycle and each part depends on the other to be complete.

"We can not break the ring." Zeff's voice trailed off. He fell into his chair and mumbled incoherent phrases to himself. His face wore the mask of a stone statue. Then he said, "And now they are coming after me again. Look! Look there! See!" He pointed to the edge of the table.

Wam rose to his feet to get a better view but saw nothing.

"The worms. They are coming after me. Look, see the big black one. He always comes first."

Wam felt completely dejected. Something had snapped in Zeff's head and he had changed from a priest stating sound theology to a babbling fool seeing invisible worms. The fears Pro described had been confirmed. Wam felt sick to his stomach and he was short of breath. Was Zeff able to bury the chieftains? Was he fit to be chief priest of Stonehenge? He realized that he must help Zeff and play a larger role at Stonehenge than he had anticipated. The great prestige of Stonehenge must not suffer because of Zeff's condition.

CHAPTER 15 MURDER ??

After two days of rest and recreation with Wam's women, Pro left Avebury and started the journey along the Icknied trail back to his clan. It was a clear fall day, cool and invigorating in the shade, yet pleasantly warm in the sun. Pro walked across tall, open fields where the tall grass was gently nodding and weaving in the breeze. He spotted a bird dancing up and down in the air as it rendered a squeaky grating song. As it sang it repeatedly fluttered its tail, showing its beautiful chestnut brown breast against black and white plumage. It's a stonechat, thought Pro. He knew the female must be nearby because stonechats mate for life. He knew that in the spring the birds build a nest with both male and female sharing the duties of raising the young. Pro thought of Qua, Ola, Oma and how the family always helped and supported each other with the chores. The thought of Qua made him feel lonely and a bit depressed, for he missed her greatly. But there was little time for feeling sad, because he knew he would see them soon. He was glad that he had contacted Wam and had gotten his cooperation. It is better for Wam to talk to Zeff than he, he thought. The two priests could make all the plans for the burials, and he felt confident that everything would work out all right.

Pro was wondering where he could stop to eat when he spotted something lying across the path several hundred paces ahead. A black object was clearly distinguishable when contrasted with the tan clay path. It looked like an animal, perhaps a bear or wolf. It was too big for a black bird. Pro stopped to study the object from a safe distance. He squinted his eyes to determine if the object was something alive or something which was moved by the breeze. He stepped on a stone to raise himself to get a better view and determined that it moved by its own power. It must be something alive, he thought. It did not behave like a wounded animal, for an animal would pull itself off the pathway and hide from predators in the bush. Pro's primitive instinct told him that this was too obvious, that it could be a trap planted on the trail. He decided to be cautious. If he approached it directly he could be easily ambushed and robbed. The Icknied Way was relatively safe compared to other trails that crisscrossed England, but there was always the possibility of renegades attacking and killing.

He threw away his walking stick and found a more substantial club-like stick that could be used as a weapon. He backtracked on the trail until the object was completely out of sight, then he left the trail and ducked down behind the safety of the high grass. He made a wide circular loop around the object watching it all the time from a distance. He darted through the waist-high grass, bending over as he ran so that he was concealed by the grass while supporting himself with his new stick. The grass smelled like freshly cut hay and the breeze made a wheezing noise when it blew through the grass which helped to conceal Pro's movements. Carefully he made his way around the object, constantly looking for signs of an ambush. Nothing suspicious or dangerous occurred so he closed in on the object instead of by passing it. He found no one hiding in the bushes or behind the trees, yet the object continued to move from time to time. Pro was curious. He did not complete the loop but he stayed in the high grass and observed the object for a good hour.

"Ooh, help me!" Pro heard weak cries and he rushed to the object when he was sure it was safe. Standing over the object, he shoved back a black woolen garment with his walking stick. He found a man bearing an old knife scar over his right cheek. He realized it was Yam.

"Yam, Yam, what is this? What happened?" He cradled Yam's head in his arms and said, "Here, here's some drink." He offered him some dandelion brew from his goat skin bag.

Pro heard faint footfalls running away from him on the clay path. He placed Yam's head back on the ground as gently as he could and stood up. He saw the figure of someone in a white cape disappear down the path. Pro was tempted to chase the figure, but Yam needed his help desperately.

"Pro." Yam's face was gray and there was a smear of blood on his side. "Oh, Pro, I've got to talk to you. It's Zeff. He has gotten worse." Yam coughed and spit up some phlegm.

Pro took off his knapsack and made a pillow for Yam as he bent down. "Here, Yam, just rest for a while before you talk."

Yam paused only to catch his breath. "Zeff doesn't want to listen ... and I don't know what he will do. I've tried ...tried to explain it to him.... many times." His speech was interrupted by short gasps for breath.

"Explain what? Yam, just slow down and tell me what it is."

"Its not my fault that he won't listen." He grabbed Pro by the shirt sleeve and pulled him down. "I can't be blamed for this. Everyone knows that I've tried. I can't be responsible. Can I?"

Pro cradled Yam's head in his arms. "I don't know, Yam, I don't know what you are talking about." Pro wanted to find where Yam was injured so he could help him but Yam felt compelled to continue.

"I have determined that the moon will be directly in front of the sun the morning of this coming summer solstice and he will not listen to it. I've checked my pole positions five times, and I know it will happen. I'm sure of it." Yam shook his head and wiped some of the perspiration from his forehead. "Zeff will not believe me. He, he doesn't want to believe me."

"I know," said Pro. "I learned of the coming eclipse at Avebury." Pro remembered that Yam was Zeff's righthand man and his responsibility was to determine when the next eclipse would occur. Within the inner circle at Stonehenge were placed two circles of wooden stakes representing the position of the sun and moon. Yam would make calculations and move the stakes a little each day. If the moon stake was positioned in front of the sun stake, it indicated an eclipse of the sun. If the sun stake was moved in front of the moon, it would indicate an eclipse of the moon.

"Yam, where are you hurt? You must rest."

"Worst of all, Zeff won't explain it to the farmers before the summer solstice," Yam went on. "He won't explain, and they will panic and riot in fear. They must be made to understand." Yam became weak, coughed some more and rested in Pro's arms. Pro placed his head gently on this knapsack and let him rest.

He finally had a chance to examine Yam as he talked. "I know of the eclipse from Wam." He adjusted his knapsack under Yam head. "Something must be done."

Yam suddenly jerked his head back and started to shiver. "Pro, you've got--," he coughed. "You've got to stop Zeff." He was shivering more and he could not talk.

"Yam, just rest for now and you can talk later." Pro wiped some of the sweat from his face and loosened his clothing around the neck. He moved his arm away from his side and discovered a gash in his rib cage oozing blood. He stripped away the clothing and wiped away the blood. He found a single gash an inch and a half long where a knife had been plunged through his chest deep into his stomach. Pro cut strips of grass that had become dry and tanned by the sun. He folded them together and made a bandage, pressing it against the wound to stop the bleeding. He looked over Yam's body for other wounds but found none. "Yam, who did this!"

Yam did not answer, his face was white, drained of all living color. "How did you get here, Yam? How did you know I would be here? Yam?" Yam lay limp like a blade of grass. Pro bent over and put his head on Yam's chest to listen to his heartbeat. He heard none. He tore back more clothing and placed his head on his bare chest. Again he heard nothing. "Dead! Yam's dead," Pro said out loud. "But why? How did this happen?" Pro pushed back the grass bandage on his chest and examined the wound again. The wound had been sliced clean. The flesh was not ripped and torn and there were no other scratches or bruises on Yam's body. Pro realized that Yam had not been killed by wild animals but had been stabbed with a knife sharp enough and long enough to penetrate deeply into his side. It could not have been done by a flint knife, for they were not long enough. It would have to have been done by a bronze knife. Pro examined further. Yam's clothing was not torn, dirty or disheveled, so he had not been roughed up in a fight either.

Pro stood and looked down at the lifeless body. "Murdered!" he said under his breath. He thought of the man in the white cape and looked at the clay pathway where he had escaped. He gritted his teeth. "Murdered without a fight and by someone he knew and trusted."

CHAPTER 16   THE BEGINNING OF THE END

On a crisp autumn morning the chiefs of the five clans who were victims of the famine met at the Nese fort to decide some very urgent matters. Several chiefs were dressed in long wool capes which were dyed a mixture of maroon, gray and gray-blue, covering them from head to foot. The capes were drawn together at the waist with a strip of rawhide. Under the garment they wore shirts and loose pants of various skins. Other chiefs wore colorful fur suits made of the skins of several different animals sewed together in a patch quilt manner. There might be a brown dog hide sewed to a gray rabbit skin which then was sewed to a black and white skunk skin. Pro wore a long wool poncho colored gray.

Two priests from Stonehenge arrived at the hill fort and joined in the meeting. They were priests that Pro had seen when he was at Stonehenge, but had never been introduced to. "We have come to help prepare the bones of the chieftains for their journey to their final resting places at clan barrows near Stonehenge. They must be ready by the feast of the major standstill of the northern moon rise, which is only 20 sunsets away," announced one priest formally.

It was true there was little time before the northern moon rise celebration, and Pro was grateful for the reinforcement in persuading the clan chiefs to do what they must do. He was annoyed, however, that the priests would just "suddenly appear" without his prior knowledge. This seemed to be Zeff's way of late, and it left Pro feeling that he was being watched and manipulated. Nevertheless, he greeted the priests warmly and introduced them to the five clan chiefs.

They all sat in a circle around the campfire, and drank warm mead and talked about farming, hunting and family. Finally the younger priest made clear the necessity for the meeting. "The bones must be buried at the Stonehenge barrows," he implored, "or you will suffer evil consequences that could come from the spirits of the dead." He presented the problem in a matter-of-fact manner, with little emotion or flair. The priests went on to explain how the bones of the chiefs must be found and the special preparation necessary. Then he reiterated the urgency of the project and stopped.

"Why should we bring the bones to Stonehenge?" asked the chief of the Efrin clan. He picked up a stray twig and flipped it on the fire. "It's not like it used to be at all; only the old go on pilgrimages to Stonehenge now." He paused and took a long swig of mead while everyone waited for him to finish.. "We will consider it, but we are too busy with the cattle now. Perhaps later in the year."

"Some of my people are leaving," said the Illa chief. "Mostly the young ones. They are going in the direction of the sunset where they can find drier weather, more food and, I guess, form a clan of their own." He stared at the dancing golden flames and extended his cold hands over the warm fire. "It will be the death of our clan, for we need the young ones here to do the hard work."

"That is a problem, a big problem, of course," said Pro, "but don't you think the bones should be buried with the proper respect for the dead?"

"Yes, you are right, Pro, but it isn't like it used to be," protested the chief of the Efrin clan. "It would be hard to find the bones of my father; I believe I could find them but it wouldn't be easy." He held his cup out towards Jep to be refilled with mead. "Yes, I believe we should bury the chief's bones at our clan barrow near Stonehenge, but it would take a lot of time away from farmin'."

"Stonehenge is where our father's fathers have been buried for a thousand summer solstices," Pro argued. "We cannot break off with that now. That would bring evil upon us. Besides, it is wrong not to bury our dead properly. Just wrong."

"I agree that the dead should be buried with respect, but we need more than 'ceremony' with the sun and moon from the Stonehenge priests," blurted the Jost chief. "My cattle are sick." He stood and waved his hands in the air and marched around the fire. "They drool and blister around the mouth. They can't eat and they lose weight and die." He looked at the other clan chiefs, who nodded understanding. "All this ceremony with the sun and moon that goes on at Stonehenge. It doesn't help. We need help; all of us need more sunshine and better weather. Can't you help us, Pro?"

Pro was familiar with the cattle disease the Jost chief was describing, but he knew of no cure. "You must keep the sick ones separated from the others and be sure they get plenty of sunshine."

The Host chief coughed, cleared his throat and began, "My wheat field has been wet and I can't work in it." He looked at the two priests from Stonehenge. "If you have so much to say about the sun and moon, why don't you tell the sun to shine? Just a few days of sunshine would dry up our fields."

Then the older priest rose to his full considerable height and solemnly intoned, "Are we no better than the rats and vermin that have eaten our dead clan people? Why do we allow our dead to die and then lie on the ground to rot like dead fish at the seashore? I tell you the gods will be angry if we don't bury our dead soon.! Has it ever occurred to you that we could be having this bad weather because the gods are already angry?"

"Maybe what you priest say is true, but someone should tell Zeff about our troubles." said the Efrin chief. All the chiefs looked at Pro. "He's your cousin, isn't he? You know him better than anyone. We want to bury our dead at Stonehenge, but need more sunshine and better crops. And we need for our cattle to get better and the young people to stay here!" All the chiefs nodded in agreement. "Can't you help us. Like you saved us during the famine?"

"I will try." Pro had not anticipated so much discontent from the clans. What he had hoped would be a simple meeting to announce the burial rites had revealed serious problems. "But you agree, we should all bury our dead at the ancestral barrows near Stonehenge, don't you? The priests need to take that message to Zeff." There was tacit consent among the chiefs as they mumbled words of agreement. Then they all stood and formed a ring around the fire, clasping hands by the wrists.

"In the name of the great ring of life, let us prepare our dead for proper burial," intoned the priests. They all raised their clasped hands high over their heads affirming their unanimity. Then they all relaxed and took a long swig of mead.

After a brief pause, Pro said, "Another thing we should talk about over the council fire is that the clans have always contributed to the priests of Stonehenge. We have always given food, wool, furs, amber, gold and other gifts and we are expected to do so now." The chiefs stopped drinking and talking and became stone silent. Only the snapping and cracking of dry wood burning in the fire could be heard. "We share some of our fall harvest with the priests every autumn equinox. We have done this for many autumns," Pro said, waiting for someone to speak up, but no one did. He shifted his body around to get more even heat from the fire, stalling for time. "The priests need food and clothing, for they are not farmers, they are priests." He shifted again to get more warmth. "The Nese clan has given bronze knives, bronze ware and some earrings and bracelets in the past and we will give them this autumn, too."

Finally the Host chief spoke out. "Food? We don't have enough food for ourselves, let alone for the priests. Some of my clan may starve this winter."

Pro protested, "I can see there is not enough food to give, but what can I tell Zeff?"

The Illa chief tapped Pro on the shoulder and said, "I've barely got enough seed for next year. Maybe I could give a special gift of some kind, some hides or something. But not food."

"My people are starving too. We can't give any of what we have." The Jost chief shrugged.

The Gott chief was briefer. "Bones, yes, food no."

The two priests exchanged glances, and then the older one rose. There was a slight stir and a few muffled mumbles as the chiefs shifted around the fire. "Zeff only asks for food and clothing and the bones of your dead chiefs. No more. The bones you have agreed to give, and that is wise of you. Even so I believe it is late, perhaps TOO LATE, to appease the gods."

"What do you mean?" asked the Gott chief.

"The god of the sun is angry. Very angry. We have had too much rain and fog, and the sun has not shone on us as it used to. He is raging, and we must sacrifice to appease him," exclaimed the younger priest.

One of the chiefs stepped forward. "But, your worship, we have had two wet seasons in a row, and surely this will pass. We have had bad weather before and it has passed. The sun god has always been good and generous with the bounty of the earth and surely will be again." His statement was only partly true for the weather had become wetter and foggier and had stayed that way longer than anyone now alive could remember.

The older priest jumped up. The muscles in his neck strained as he said, "In the past, the clans buried their dead at the Stonehenge barrows without being reminded to do so. In the past, the clans gave food and clothing to the priests without being reminded to do so. We did not have to ask. In the past, the gods were good to everyone but now, you have erred and you have failed the gods." He paused and paced around the fire. His voice had become high pitched and strained. "Who ever told you that you should pile your clansman bones on the other side of the river? Just dump them there!' He pointed directly at the Efrin chief. "And then forget all about them? Such blasphemy! A curse you have caused for all of us."

The second priest jumped to his feet and shouted, "The priests at Stonehenge know that the gods are angry and that they can be vengeful. You must give more than your fair ration of food, along with the bones of your chief, or something tragic will come to pass." Both priests threw their capes on the ground and paraded around the fire, stomping their feet and jumping on and off the capes.

The chiefs had never seen the priests in such a rage before. "What will come to pass?" they asked, talking all at once.

The younger priest stopped, leaned over, cupped his hand to his mouth and whispered, "The sun!" Then he continued parading around the fire. He would jump up and down, shout and clap his hands. "It will be the sun!"

Then the parading stopped as abruptly as it began and all the chiefs asked, "The sun? What do you mean, the sun?" The older priest stood erect and slowly proclaimed in a loud clear voice raising his arms up to the heavens. "The sun will disappear completely unless each clan gives generously."

"My people will starve!" shouted the Host chief. "It will be just like the famine all over again. We can't do this!"

"You must! It will be worse if the sun disappears. Zeff will try to stop the sun from disappearing, but he needs our help," corrected the Jost chief.

"The sun will disappear! I can't believe it," said one chief.

"You must believe it. The sun WILL disappear."

There was more muttering under the breath among the chiefs. The Gott chief stood away from the confusion of the crowd while he contemplated. At first he was very suspicious of what the priests were saying, for he had never seen the sun completely obscured in his lifetime. What the priests were saying was unbelievable. On the other hand, he thought, the priests from Stonehenge had never come to their camp fire before. Was this really that urgent? he questioned to himself. Would the sun really disappear? He rubbed the side of his chin. Would I dare give the priests a sick cow that will probably die anyway?

"It has been determined that if the gods are not appeased the sun will disappear after mid-summer," one priest announced in a pontifical manner.

Pro was watching the whole scene, quietly disassociated from any participation. He knew the priests were referring to the eclipse of the sun at the summer solstice. Pro thought of Yam's murder by the side of the trail and Wam's insisting that the farmers should be made to understand the eclipse so they would not be afraid when it occurred. Then he thought of what was happening now -- fear and bribery and forcing starving people to give.

"But we need the sunlight to dry our fields. We can't work the fields covered with mud," said the Jost chief.

"Yes, if there is one thing we need now it is more sunshine," added the Host chief.

"More sun?" The priests became frenzied. They ran around the fire shouting, "How can you ask for more sun when the sun gods are already angry?" They kicked some dirt on the fire. They spat on the chiefs and then cursed them. "You must bring more than your food ration to Stonehenge, and sacrifice more! Zeff and Wam will be violent if you don't. There is little they can do if you don't help."

"We will help. We will bring more food. We will bring more food!" the chiefs replied in a dispirited response.

The priests were satisfied, so they picked up their capes, threw them over their shoulders and marched back to Stonehenge leaving behind a frightened and bewildered, but committed, group of farmers.

CHAPTER 17 THE CIRCLE OF DEATH AND LIFE

The major standstill of the moon rise in the north occurs once in 12 moon cycles or every 112 years. The uncommon occurrence of this moon rise is the reason that there is a very special festival which typically lasts three days. On the first day several representatives of each clan would place the gifts of food at the heel stone, while other members of the clan would prepare their ancestral barrow for the interrment of their chiefs. On the second day the actual ceremony of consecration of the dead would be performed over the bones presented at the clan barrow. The actual sighting of the rare moon rise would occur on the third day. After feast and celebration, the pilgrims will bid their friends and relatives goodbye and start the long walk back to their homes. The time for the celebration had come, and the ceremony had been carefully planned by Zeff and Wam.

Representatives of the five clans were carrying food for gifts and the bones of their departed chiefs to Stonehenge. They were bewildered and uncertain pilgrims who carefully made their way to the heel stone site. They shivered in the predawn cold as they waited for a priest to arrive. "Is this the way you present gifts to the priests?" asked one. "I have never been to this fertility rite before."

"I don't think so; I think we must bow and chant, or do something. I wish a priest would help us."

"Do you think the sun will really disappear?"

"That's what the priest said."

"He said it would reappear again if we give enough gifts." They fell to their knees and bowed as they left their gifts. Some left leather satchels and sheaths for knives. Others left bushels of oats, wheat, acorns, mushrooms, and live cattle both fat and lean. The cattle were small, only four feet at the shoulder and looked more like large dogs. The Nese clan gave sheets of linen for clothing that Pro had obtained from merchants while trading on the north coast. The Nese clan also gave bronze knives, nose rings and breast pins, and ten baskets of beans.

They waited, and no priest appeared to bless them.

Other pilgrims came and commenced to chant, "Ah la,la, kay, oh hew ki mun ba." They repeated the chant over and over in a high-pitched tone as they approached the heel stone. The pilgrims had been traveling for two days and were road weary and suffered from hunger. Baskets of apples, barley, linseed and hazel nuts were hauled in, also pottery and wool blankets removed from their backs. No one knew exactly how to present their gifts so they laid them in a meticulous straight row in front of the heel stone.

Still no priest appeared.

The pilgrims were frightened and uncertain. They sang louder and some gave more gifts. All the time their hearts were pounding in their chests as they wondered if they had given enough to stop the sun from disappearing. Fires were made and burning incense filled the air with the odor of rose.

Finally, at first light, a priest in a white robe appeared from behind the altar stone. He elevated himself on a rise where he could see the large numbers of pilgrims milling about. A smile appeared across his lips when he saw the gifts accumulating at the heel stone. He nodded to his bell ringer to begin the ceremony. The bell ringer struck a large brass cymbal which immediately alerted the pilgrims to face the great horseshoe and to fall on their knees and bow. Four more times the bell ringer struck the bell and the sound fully resonated through the crowd. Five rings meant that this was an exclusive meeting presided over only by the chief priest. In the cool, moist morning air, the sound carried far and wide, and the whole countryside stopped what they were doing, counted five rings and knew that Zeff was presiding.

Zeff stood at the altar stone in the middle of the Stonehenge circle -- the holiest part of Stonehenge, a section where only the high priests could go. There were five priests altogether, each busy behind the altar stone burning incense or chanting. When Zeff raised his hands, the poncho-like albino sheep skin robe fell open, draping down from his arms. All the priests stopped what they were doing and faced the pilgrims gathered around the heel stone. When all was quiet Zeff intoned his blessing.

"God of the fertility, God of the sun, we accept these gifts from thy earth.

I am the pregnant seed engendered by the great wild ox.

I am the great storm that goes forth,

I am the lord of the land,

61

I am the chief of all chieftains, the father of all the lands,

I am the big brother of the gods, who brings full prosperity,

I am the record keeper of heaven and earth,

I am he who directs justice with the sky-god,

I am he who decrees the fates with the sky-god."

While he talked, his assistants circulated among the pilgrim worshipers noting what everyone gave and how generous they were.

Zeff continued, "In this time of the fall harvest we will chose a maiden who will represent the earth-goddess. We will choose a virile young man who will impregnate the earth-goddess maiden, then he will be sacrificed to the dark side of the moon. The earth-goddess will decline in favor in the winter, but in the spring she will appear in full readiness to bring forth her newborn and begin the next fertility ring." He spread his hands out and looked up to the heavens. "This is the way of the animals in the forest. This is the way of the birds in the sky. This is the way of the fish in the streams. This is the way of the seeds in the ground. And this is the way of the great ring religion of Stonehenge." Then he stepped down from his elevated position and announced, "Tomorrow we must go to the clan barrows and bury the departed chiefs. We will bury the chief of the Nese clan first." Then Zeff stood in front of each clan's offering, blessing their gifts and thanking the clan representatives.

Pro and Jep were standing aloof at a distance and had a different interpretation of Zeff's harvest ceremony. Pro whispered to Jep, " Did you hear what I heard?"

"It sounds as if he is talking about sacrificing someone."

"Yes, that's what I heard too," said Pro.

"Zeff will choose a man to seduce some maiden, and then he will kill the man," Jep continued.

"And what man will Zeff choose?" asked Pro.

"His enemy, of course," added Jep. They exchanged sober glances

"His enemy or one who knows too much about the eclipse, Jep." Pro firmly grabbed Jep by the arm and stopped him abruptly from walking. "Jep, we must keep a close eye on Zeff. We must know ahead of time who the man will be. I think Zeff is a dangerous, sick man. Jep, you go, and keep close to Zeff and his priests. Tomorrow, at the burial of my father, let me know what you have learned."

"But we must keep silent at the funeral."

"True, we'll have to communicate with hand signals. If you have learned that I am the man chosen, stand with your arms folded across your chest. If someone else is the man, clasp your hands in prayer. And if Zeff hasn't decided yet just stand with your hands hanging down." He released his firm grip of Jep's arm, and they nodded and departed.

CHAPTER 18 THE FUNERAL

The bones of the dead chieftains had been carefully and ceremoniously prepared for burial days before the time of the ceremony. The bones had been picked clean of all flesh and placed on a skin of a sheep in the open ground to see what birds or animals might be attracted to them. The type of animal that the bones attracted gave a spiritual meaning to the clan family of the departed. If, for example, a fox had been attracted by the bones, then the gods of the next world considered the deceased to be clever or cunning.

A hobby, a falcon-like bird about the size of a pheasant, perched on Gor's bones briefly. It was a handsome bird with blue gray wing feathers, white chest with black dots and reddish tail. He flew from the bones and caught a bat flying nearby. The hobby took the bat high in the sky, commenced tumbling, wildly gliding upside-down, looping the loop as he passed the bat to his mate while both were in flight. It was a daring courtship ceremony of a bird in full command and an excellent omen for Gor, a man who was always in full command. The Nese clan was very pleased and satisfied with this fine omen.

The bones of the chieftain were bleached white in the sunlight. The center core of the long leg bones and arm bones were cleaned out, holes were punched in them at the right places to make crude flutes and whistles.

The barrow was prepared early too. It had been twelve summer solstices since Pro's grandfather was buried and the huge portal stone had settled firmly in place. Six priests pushed and pulled and finally coaxed the stone away. A dank and fetid odor hung heavily over the barrow entrance. The priests crawled into the cenotaph to examine the bones of Pro's grandfather. They found dirt had fallen and had covered the bones of a pet goat that was buried near the side of the skeleton. A shiny gold cup was found slightly out of the reach of his right hand bone, and an amber medallion with the image of an entombed spider remained around his neck bone. Rats had invaded the chamber and had done much damage. Parts of the skeleton had been scattered about and were not aligned in the proper burial order. A priest removed the rat's nest and placed the old bones off to the side, making room for the new bones. When all was ready inside the cenotaph, the priests left the chamber and covered the entrance with a gray linen blanket.

Now the burial ceremony was ready to begin and all the Nese clan walked slowly, two abreast, to the barrow entrance. Mott walked on the left carrying the skeleton remains cradled in his arms like a baby. Across from him was Pro, who cradled a crushed skull in his arms. Pro looked at Mott and said, "I don't like this, carrying these bones." Behind Pro were Ola and Oma, who carried the skeleton of a little dog that was Gor's pet. Others followed each carrying something that had been important to Gor during his lifetime. One carried a bowl of honey, someone else carried a bowl of mixed berries, another carried a bronze dagger. In the background the priests were playing bone flutes, whistles, drums and a ram's horn. There was no melody or beat to the music, just loud noises intended to scare away any evil spirits. A bleached white linen blanket was spread at the entrance to the tomb. Each member of the clan knelt down, one at a time, and placed their tribute on the blanket. Then the family all knelt at the end of the blanket in silence.

Pro glanced at Jep, but did not get eye contact.

"Oh ra tar ra oh la," chanted Zeff in a deep baritone voice and the other priests joined. "We must drive the dead spirits out. We must force them out," Zeff said. A priest paraded around the blanket, flinging red ocher dust on the skeletons and on the family. At times he indiscriminately threw the dust high, and the whole party was obscured in a red cloud.

Pro worried how he could get Jep's signal if he couldn't see him.

The noise from the musical instruments continued in a gradual crescendo. Another priest had started a fire, and at specified intervals he would throw a powder into the fire that would cause a loud sound and burst into blinding red flames. At those times the chant would be sung and the instruments played with a greater loudness, frightening everyone. The ceremony continued for an hour.

Then, suddenly all the noise and confusion stopped. Zeff proclaimed, "All the evil spirits have departed. It is time for burial." Zeff went into the cenotaph to the spot where Gor's bones were to be placed. He knelt down and carefully laid each bone in a prescribed order. The skeleton was placed on its left side in a crouched position facing the southeast towards the raising sun. "As the rising sun is the beginning of a new day in the live world, so it begins a day in the hereafter." The hands of the skeleton were folded in front and a bright bronze dagger was placed at his side. Zeff's assistant priest followed with the bones of the pets that had been laid out on the blanket. They were placed beside Gor just as they had been outside on the blanket.

While Zeff and the other priests were busy inside the cenotaph, Pro caught Jep's eye. Jep was kneeling on the linen blanket; he stood straight and allowed his hands to fall down his sides.

A hot concoction of whiting eels, frogs, toads, snakes, mice, hares and shrews was poured into a pottery bowl and placed at Gor's skull. There was also some bread, onions, turnips and small bits of meat for the dog. A nutritious green plant called 'goose foot' was spread out by his side. Pro didn't know the exact purpose of this, but it had been at every burial ceremony.

When the ceremony was over, the heavy portal stone was rolled back into the shallow depression at the entrance to the barrow. The stone fell snugly into place and sealed the entrance tighter than had concrete been used. Zeff motioned for everyone to kneel. "Gor has passed on the black side of the moon in death," he said. "He will come back in the full of the moon again in due course." Zeff faced the portal stone. "Bow your head and close your eyes in prayer." Everyone did as Zeff instructed. "This barrow is empty, for Gor is somewhere else. This barrow is a mystical gateway through which life starts anew and where the living and the dead meet." The priests repeatedly threw handfuls of red ocher dust in the air creating a cloud so thick that the kneeling Nese clan could not see their hands in front of their faces. When the dust settled, Zeff and the other priests were gone.

Pro and Mott rose from their kneeling position and brushed the dust off their shoulders and exchanged glances. "He didn't notice, did he?" said Mott.

Pro checked over his shoulder. There was no one listening. "No, he didn't." He smiled with a sense of satisfaction. "And he will never know now, and we won't have to worry about it." Mott smiled back, nodded his head and said no more. The bones placed in the cenotaph were those of Pro's mother. Gor's bones were still in the barrow at the fort fulfilling Pro's father's solemn death bed request.

Pro met with Qua, Ola and Oma and they immediately left for the hill fort, telling only Jep. He would be two days away if Zeff decided to choose him as the man to seduce the maiden.

The ceremony for the major standstill of the moon rise in the north occurred the next day at the southern rim of Stonehenge. It had rained continually since early morning, and there was no sign of the skies clearing up. The pilgrims stood barefoot in mud up to their ankles. Their shoes consisted of sheets of soft leather which wrapped around their feet, stuffed with straw at the sole and tied together at the ankle. The shoes were useless in the mud so they were removed, tied together by leather shoe strings, and draped around their necks. The shoes were saved for the more strenuous trip back to their homes. They huddled under makeshift lean-tos of skins and bark, trying to keep warm and dry by rubbing their arms and shoulders vigorously. "How can we possibly see the moon rise in this kind of weather?" asked a Jost farmer.

"Oh, maybe Zeff can make it stop raining, then clear away all the clouds, and then we'll see it," said a Illa farmer with sarcasm.

"What would happen it we just left?" asked a women

"Oh, we wouldn't dare do that. At least until we are told to by the priests."

Zeff and Wam were sitting in the shelter that contained the clay tablets of Stonehenge, eating a roasted duck. "Are all the gifts gathered and out of the rain," Zeff asked.

"Yes, they were put away last night," said Wam.

"We took in enough food to last quite a while." A confident smile came across Zeff's face. "We had to force them to give by frightening them with the eclipse, you know."

"Yes, I know," Wam agreed. He was eating a drumstick he had pulled off the roast duck

"We would not have gotten all this food, which, of course, we desperately need." He stopped and pointed towards the heel stone. "We had to have the food. It was absolutely necessary." Zeff rubbed his hands together and smiled triumphantly.

"Yes, I know." Wam took a generous bite of the duck drumstick.

"Sometimes it is necessary to use the knowledge given us by the gods to get things done. To force them to give what they are obligated to give."

Zeff waited for Wam to finish but Wam was busy pulling some meat off the drumstick with his fingers. Finally he looked up. "Yes, that's true."

"Only a few priests have the knowledge of the eclipses, you know. The god of the sun does not share that kind of knowledge with farmers. For one thing, they would never understand, no matter how much you tried to tell them, and they are, really, better off not knowing."

"Yes. That's true," Wam acknowledged as he licked his fingers clean. "Wait, that's not true. Some of the people know about the eclipses."

Zeff looked hard at Wam. "What do you mean? How could they? We priests don't even know why it happens."

"Yes, that's true. It is mysterious."

"Who are you talking about? How could anyone outside the priesthood know about the eclipses?" Zeff demanded.

"Well, Pro knows. Pro, the trader of the Nese clan, he knows. I explained it to him when he visited me at Avebury. He understands." Wam picked over the tray of roast duck and found a wing.

Zeff looked off into space and thought, "Of course, Pro would know. He travels all over the plain from Cornwall to Marlborough Downs. He talks to everyone and knows the shaman of every clan. He would know if anyone knew." Zeff smoothed his beard in a nervous gesture. Could one man, one lone voice, ruin this for me? He shook his head in thought. "Is he the only one you have explained this to?"

"Yes, the only one." He placed the wing down, wiped the grease from his hand and drank some mead.

"That's good," smiled Zeff. He held open the flap on the tent and observed the rain. "But if he did talk, what then?"

"I don't know," mumbled Wam. "We have a lot at risk, here, but it was all necessary, using the eclipse, I mean."

It was raining harder now, and raindrops played an almost deafening tattoo on the skin roof of Zeff's hut. There was a pause as Zeff examined the duck to find the other drumstick. "The one chosen to impregnate the harvest goddess... have we chosen him?" Zeff asked in a voice barely audible.

"Why, yes. You told the clans after the last chief was buried. It was Reo the farmer from the Illa clan. Don't you remember?"

"Oh, yes, I remember, of course," said Zeff. Zeff nervously tapped his fingers on the table. "Have we ever had two candidates for that honor?"

"No, never. The gods never demanded it."

Zeff thought, Maybe it would not be necessary to silence Pro. He is only one person and he could not affect all the clans. Besides, he is my cousin, and, he would not do anything to destroy me. It's not his nature. Zeff said, "Well, then, overall, things are getting better. I feel more comfortable with the chiefs buried here at last."

"Ah, yes, it's been good. Perhaps we can get back to normal again."

"Yes."

"Maybe the sun god will bless us with more sunshine and warmth." No sooner had Zeff spoken when he heard a loud, ear-piercing clap of thunder. Zeff looked at Wam and both wondered if the gods had spoken through the thunder. Zeff laughed, and said, "It is nothing. There has been thunder and lighting all day."

"It doesn't mean that the gods are angry with us," said Wam.

"No, it doesn't." But they both were silent for a moment "It's just thunder along with the rain."

"Yes. I've seen it happen many times," confirmed Wam. "But we don't have a clear sky to see the moon rise." Zeff pulled the flap back on the door and saw the rain coming down in streaks. "It's past the time of the moon rise. I guess we should tell the peasants to go back to their homes." Zeff sat in silence for a moment and finally asked, "Wam, would you tell the peasants?"

Wam agreed and he put his cape over his head, tied it tight around the neck and left.

When he was sure Wam had left and all was quiet, Zeff mumbled, "The gods still hate me." He pulled the tarp back and again a steady rain continued. "They caused it to rain on this day. Why? This moon rise will not happen again in my life time. Never! And it had to rain." He thought back. "It rained in four of the last seven ceremonies of the sun and moon. The gods do hate me." He began to moan and cry. "Oh no, not again." He looked at the mead bowl and saw some movement at the top. "No, not this." He saw black worms slowly crawling out the top and down the sides of the vase.

CHAPTER 19   THE STORM BEFORE THE STORM

Pro resumed the tin trading with Cornwall. His concern about Zeff's mental state never left his mind, and Pro made inquiries about Zeff at every trading stop. His intentions were to stay away from Stonehenge and hope for the best for Zeff. He learned that Reo did seduce the young maiden under the five arches at Stonehenge as planned. Reo was then killed by a knife wound inflicted by Zeff and the other priests. Pro felt safe from that threat.

That winter Pro and his trading party were returning from Cornwall with their boats filled with cassiterite ore when they were caught in a terrible snow and wind storm. The river Avon, which was normally calm and navigable, was choppy with jagged waves that challenged Pro's boatman at every turn. The water penetrated their thin garments, chilling them to the bone. The icy snow came down hard and would sting their exposed cheeks and foreheads like little darts. Two boats, filled to the top with the heavy cassiterite, had capsized, and two crewmen were drowned. Their bodies were claimed by the deep water and never surfaced. The other boats were pulled along the bank where some of the ore was unloaded, making the boats safer and more buoyant. Every person in the trading party had fallen in the river at least once and all were wet and shivering in the cold. They were saturated with water, mud and river slime and their clothing clung to their bodies like lead weights.

They desperately needed the warmth from a fire but found the dead wood covered with snow and wet. Finally, dry dead limbs and twigs were stripped from standing pin oak trees for fuel. Some dried oak leaves left over from the summer season were stubbornly clinging to an oak tree and were used for kindling. A site was chosen along the raised embankment on the river which offered some protection from the cold wind and snow. A fire was born with flint sparks darting into the oak leaves. When a flame was produced, twigs and limbs were added and gradually precious heat was produced. One fire was not enough and a second one was made seven or eight feet from the first. Pro and his crew stripped off most of their wet clothing and kept warm by standing between the two fires. They fastened the wet clothing to poles and extended them over the fires to dry. When all the crew had dried out and had a bit to eat, they continued the journey to the Nese hill fort.

It had stormed continuously for several days, piling snow in every opening on the landscape. Snow drifts had formed like sand dunes and the wind was ugly at times, gusting in hurricane proportions, indiscriminately uprooting many trees and destroying many farm huts. Farmers and farm animals were helplessly exposed to the weather.

The only sign of life that Pro found when he arrived at the Nese fort was from the hut of Mott. Gray smoke was streaking through his thatched roof, changing directions at the whim of the wind. Pro's bedraggled group arrived and were immediately treated like heroes. "Pro, Qua, Jep, you made it. You are alive and safely back," said Mott as he greeted them. "You look like you need this." He handed each a generous bowl of hot dandelion brew and a hot, pasty maroon colored gruel of goat's blood, ground oats and linseed. A salt stone was passed around and all of Pro's group took a lick.

"A toast," said Pro as he held the bowl over his head. "It's good to get back - alive, and it's good to see everyone here." Everyone cheered, hugged and greeted each other. More hot dandelion brew was provided because it heated their insides clear down to the pits of their stomachs. Everyone wore several layers of skins and woolen garments, but they still were cold. The wind whistled through the thin loose walls of the hut at will.

The celebration stopped when someone shouted, "Ros, where's my brother, Ros?" A frail women approached Pro. "Where's Ros?" All eyes turned to Pro as he told the tragic details of the boat capsizing in the river Avon and the loss of two men, Ros and Fam. He told of their heroism in an effort to save the boats and the cargo and paid tribute to their memory. Their story would be retold at clan gatherings in subsequent years and become a legend. The Nese clan was small, and the loss of two able men would be felt by all. All the clan members would go to the families of Ros and Fan and offer help and comfort. All offered assurance that special care would be given to the children.

"Where's Dun?" inquired Jep. "How's she getting along with the baby?" He scanned the whole hut thinking maybe she was standing behind someone. The clan again became quiet, and Mott stood up, straightened out his coat and explained. "Dun is gone. She left several days ago." He walked directly in front of Jep and placed his hands on his shoulders. "She had to leave, Jep. She had to leave because there was trouble with the Efrins."

"Trouble? What kind of trouble?" asked Jep. "What do you mean 'she's gone?'"

"Remember Stav, son of Terr in the Efrin clan? He was always trying to flirt with Dun. You know, get her attention."

Jep's face grew tense, and he wiggled loose from Mott's hold. "Isn't Slav the Efrin who is loony?-- the one who never got well after the famine? The one who does strange things?" Jep made a hard fist out of his hands and stood in a pugnacious position. "What did he do to her, Mott? Tell me exactly what he did to her. He was always hanging around her, bothering her."

"Stop. Let me finish, Jep." Mott put his hands back on Jep's shoulders. "Don't get mad. You'll be proud of Dun when I'm finished." Jep backed off, looked Mott in the eye and released his tight fists. Mott continued, "Well, Slav kept talking and teasing her, but she would have none of it, Jep. Finally, she told him to stop. And he wouldn't, so she got so angry that she hit him in the face with her fists and gave him a bloody nose."

"A bloody nose," repeated Jep. "She really hit him that hard?" Jep snickered, he always thought of his mate as petite, even frail, one who needed his protection, not someone who could clobber a man in the nose.

"She really gave him a blow and the blood was smeared all over his face. She hit him hard." A smile of satisfaction came over Mott's face. "She never gave in to Slav, Jep. She was true to the end."

"But why is she gone now?" Jep fidgeted with his bowl of dandelion brew, spilling half of it on the dirt floor. "She's big with child, really big. Why did she have to leave?"

"Well, Slav was embarrassed in front of his own people, being hit by a women and all," Mott said. "And some of his own people teased him even though Terr, Slav's father, tried to stop them. Slav wanted to get even. So he found a way to get to Dun. He told her that he ate her father during the famine, and Dun really got upset at that. Every time Slav saw Dun he would say the same thing over and over again. Terr tried to stop that too, but he couldn't. The more Slav told her he ate her father, the more upset Dun became. Finally, just a few days ago, she couldn't help herself and she picked up a big rock and crashed it on Slav's head. It, well, it killed him."

"It killed him!" repeated Pro. A heavy silence came over the clan, interrupted only by the whining of the wind outside. The gravity of the moment held everyone spellbound.

"What, what happened next?" demanded Jep.

"She came running to the fort, told me what happened, then packed her knapsack and left."

"Great god of fertility - she is due to have her baby before the next full moon," said Qua. "We must help her somehow. Where is she?"

"And in this cold snow and wind. She can't live outside. Where can we help her?" asked a women from the clan.

"What about the Efrins?" asked Pro.

"The Efrins, well -- the last we heard, they didn't want a blood killing. Terr doesn't want revenge. They will be coming here as soon as the storm breaks and we will know for sure. In a way I'm glad that Dun is gone away so the Efrins can't get her. If they wanted her, she would not have a chance."

The clan folk slowly returned to the business of keeping warm. They huddled close together and vigorously rubbed each other on their backs and shoulders. More wood was put on the fire and more hot dandelion brew was served. Pro made his way through the crowd to Mott and stood close behind him. He leaned forward and whispered in his ear. "Where did Dun go? I know you know."

Mott said "I can never keep a secret from you." He put his hand over his mouth and whispered, "I believe she went to Stonehenge."

In a few days' time the storm passed and the sun shown brightly, warming the countryside. The Nese fort had some unexpected visitors when three priests from Stonehenge came to see Pro. "We bid you greetings from Zeff, the chief priest of Stonehenge," the spokesman said. "Zeff wishes to see you. Stonehenge has been damaged by the storm and he needs your counsel immediately."

"Needs my counsel?" Pro said. He knew that this could well be a trap, to get him to come to Stonehenge and then capture or kill him. Then there were Ola and Oma, who were now of age. Zeff has had his lecherous eye on them. No, the last person that Pro wanted to contact was Zeff, whom he felt he couldn't trust. "Why does he want my counsel?"

"A large stone lintel has fallen off one of the uprights of the great circle and needs to be repaired immediately. It has fallen to the ground and is broken in many pieces."

"Lintel? What's a lintel?" asked Pro.

"A lintel is the stone that lies on top the archway."

"But, I know nothing about repairing stone lintels. I trade in bronze. "He pointed to his brother. "He is a bronze smith, and we know nothing about the stones at Stonehenge."

"Zeff knows that you are very knowledgeable, and you trade with many people and are informed on many matters. He feels that you would know how to arrange the repair of the lintel better than anyone." The priest bowed slightly and smiled and added, "He is desperate and needs you."

Pro was impressed that Zeff thought so highly of him. In fact he was flattered, but he also knew that being flattered might be the first step to being trapped. "I don't know how I could help." Pro shrugged his shoulders and looked helpless.

"Stonehenge is build so solidly that it took the worst possible storm in many winter solstices to damage it," said the priest. "That is what we had at Stonehenge two days ago." He looked around at the debris that the storm had scattered about. "I see that you had a bad storm here too."

"Yes, we did." Pro remembered the capsizing of his ore boats and the loss of two men. It was the worst snow and wind storm that he ever remembered.

"Well, Zeff would like to counsel with you."

The priest was insistent, and Zeff was still the chief priest. Finally Pro said, "There is a family of masons who are good at stone working. There are two brothers from the Jost clan near Marlborough Downs; I believe their names are Una and Vor. We will go to the Jost clan, and get Una and Vor, and go to Stonehenge and let them tell us how to fix the lintel. That's the only thing I know to do."

The priests agreed that they would start the journey the following morning. As they walked away Pro thought, "Is Zeff so out of touch with the craft trades that he can't find the right help himself? Or is he loonier than ever and has he lost confidence in his judgment?

"Is it safe, Pro? Can you trust Zeff?" shouted Mott. "I don't think you should go."

Pro thought for a minute. "Oh, yes Mott, I'll take my entire trading party of eight along." He smiled. "We'll have more men than Zeff has priests. If he starts trouble, we'll fight." His jaw was firm and he was determined not to let Zeff trick him.

"But Ola and Oma will stay here with their mother."

CHAPTER 20 THE MEANING BEHIND THE LINTEL

Pro's trading party arrived late in the morning and set up camp in the meadow called "the avenue" which is outside Stonehenge. Pro was met by a priest at his camp site. "Zeff would like for you to come directly to the fallen lintel and meet with him."

"I have brought two expert stone masons with me so we can be certain what we must do," said Pro.

The priest didn't know exactly what to say. "You know that it is necessary to have special permission to enter the inner circle of Stonehenge. I must get permission from Zeff." He hurried off.

"Tell Zeff that we know how important it is to repair the lintel and we can determine what must be done before this day is over only with the expert help of the masons."

Soon the priest appeared and waved Pro and the masons into the inner court at the site of the damage. As Pro left, he said to Jep. "Keep an eye on me all the time. If there is any rough play, come charging with the whole trading party. If I think there is going to be trouble, I will raise my right hand in the air, like this." Pro raised his right arm high in the air over his head.

"But it's a holy shrine. We aren't permitted to come in," protested Jep.

"Keep an eye on me and watch my every move -- you come in it I need you." Pro's eyes were locked in Jep's. "You come in! There is no knowing what Zeff might do."

The perfect circle of stones with their smooth platform lintel tops had not been disrupted since it was built five hundred summer solstices before. It was an awesome monument of massive stone archways; a glorified shrine to the people of Salisbury Plain for as long as anyone could remember. The fallen lintel created a catastrophic void, a grievous gap in the structure that was immediately noticed. The immense lintel had fallen to the ground at the base of the circle, disjointed and broken in three big pieces.

Zeff was standing beside the stone tapping it with his walking stick. After briefly greeting Pro, he said, "As you can see, it has to be repaired as soon as possible. We can't have this break in the sacred stone circle. It is irreverent; it just can't be."

The masons recognizing the urgency displayed by Zeff immediately went to work. They produced many narrow strips of soft leather which they used in making measurements. They crawled on their hands and knees checking the cracks and gaps in the stones and making careful measurements.

"Could I have a ladder? asked Una. Zeff hastily motioned to his assistant, and a ladder was produced made of two sturdy limbs with cross steps of branches tied in for steps. Una climbed to the top of the stone circle where the lintel had been and dropped a plumb line down to the ground. He tied a knot in the leather plumb line, marking the distance. "This lintel stone fell the distance of two and a half standing men," he said in amazement. "No wonder it broke into three pieces."

"We can see that," Zeff said to Pro in a belittling tone. "What about the knobs?" He pointed to the top of the circle. "The tenons, as you call them, on top of the uprights. Are they damaged?" He fidgeted with his walking stick and continued to tap.

The lintel did not simply rest on top of the upright, but was held in place by a pair of projecting knobs or tenons, and the knobs had to fit into holes perfectly aligned in the stone lintel. Una measured and examined the tenons, tying knots in leather strings. "The tenons are fine, not damaged at all, and we can use them again."

"Good," Zeff shouted back. He increased the tempo and loudness of his tapping with his walking stick. "This is terrible, Pro, just terrible. You've got to help me."

"Vor," Una called to his brother, who was busy on the ground measuring, "this has two mortise-and-tenon joints like the carpenters use. The tenon is the width of my hand extended and as deep as my hand closed. So we'll have to grind a hole in the new lintel stone at the exact place to cap over the tenons."

"I know," said Vor. "I'll measure the mortise hole down here."

"This lintel is rectangular in shape, Vor, but it curves on its inner and outer faces so that they follow the curve of the big circle," Una told Vor. "It's going to be a hard thing to make."

"And the distance across the circle is about twenty paces," interrupted Zeff. "And you had better get that curve in the lintel right so it makes a tight fit with the other lintels, because that has to connect to make the perfect sacred ring." Zeff turned to Pro. "This is the circle of life and cannot be broken. We've got to have this repaired before the great feast of the summer solstice. The farmers would not understand."

"Understand what, Zeff?" Pro asked. He thought maybe Zeff would unintentionally say something about the eclipse of the sun and maybe a word about the murder of Yam. Pro noticed that Zeff was constantly moving, twitching and fingering his walking stick or his beard. Pro thought that now was a good time to ask a few questions. "Say, Zeff, I haven't seen Yam, your chief assistant today. How is he?" Pro studied Zeff's eyes to catch any facial gesture or body movement that might betray him.

"Oh. he's gone. He left three moons ago. It's strange, too, I don't know where he went." Zeff looked directly into Pro's eyes. "I miss him-- it's strange, I really miss him." Pro knew from boyhood days that Zeff's reaction seemed genuine and that he could not bluff his way out of this. But then, if he was affected by the moon's rays he would say and do many strange things. Pro pondered, who was the person in the white cape who ran off into the woods when Pro found Yam on the Icknied Way? Only Zeff had a white cape which was made from an albino deer skin.

Their talk was interrupted when Una called out, "Vor, here's another thing-- the lintels are jointed to their neighbors by tongue-and-groove joints just like the carpenters use. It's a perfect fit. It is almost impossible for these stones to move back and forth up here. They are all laid perfectly level, too."

Una came down from the circle top and went off to the side to confer with Vor. They both went to the fallen lintel, spit on the stone, and rubbed in the saliva with another stone. Vor then rubbed his hand across the wet spot and looked at the residue. "Ah yes, it is just as I thought, It's sarsen stone from Marlborough Downs."

Finally the two masons came before Pro and Zeff with strips of leather draped over their backs. Vor said, "We have finished our examining and measuring and have determined what must be done. The lintel measures about the length of two men's arm fully spread out from the shoulders." Una spread both his arm out to demonstrate. "It is the width from my chin to my extended finger tips and the thickness of my armpit to my extended finger tips." Una carefully laid each strip of knotted leather across the ground with the appropriate measurements for Zeff to inspect.

Zeff toyed with several of the leather strips with his walking stick, pushing them back and forth on the ground. Finally he asked, "How long will it take to rebuild the lintel and put it back in place?"

"That depends on how quickly we find a stone we can work with at Marlborough Downs. We may find a stone, work it to the measurements we've determined here." Vor pointed to the leather strips. "But it could split when we grind the holes for the mortise and tenon fittings. That's grinding across the grain, which could fracture the stone. Too much pressure would cause it to split. You know now hard sarsen stone is to work with?" He waited for Zeff to ask. Zeff didn't. "It's the hardest stone there is. You can only use other sarsen stone to grind it."

Neither Pro nor Zeff knew a thing about sarsen stone, and they looked at each other with blank stares.

"It could split when we make the groove for the tongue and groove fitting, or size it for the exact curve that fits in the circle," added Una. "It could split wide open; we would have to start all over again."

"We need a perfect fit on top. We may have to grind to size three or four times before we make a successful lintel," said Vor.

"And making it level," Una continued, "that has to be done by hand grinding after we get it on top of the circle. That will take--."

"Stop! Stop it!" shouted Zeff. "I don't want to hear any more about how difficult it will be. All I want to know is when you can finish it! No, wait... I will tell you when I want this to be finished." Zeff stepped forward, stretched to his full stature and pointed to the fallen lintel with his walking stick. "A new lintel, like this one, has to be in place on top of the circle before the next summer solstice." Then Zeff stopped. There was complete silence, and Zeff turned his back on the masons and walked away.

Vor, Una and Pro exchanged rigid, steely glances. Finally Vor broke the silence and said to Pro in a confidential, professional tone, "We can't possibly finish this by the coming summer solstice." He shook his head. "It will take four, maybe five summer solstices to do all the work. And we will need men, many men. After we find the right stone, we must grind it to size and move it from Marlborough Downs on log rollers to Stonehenge. That will take a lot of men. Then we've got to build a log platform and raise it to the top of the pillars step by step. And when we get to the top of the circle, we must grind some more to place it for an exact fit. All that will take time, much time, and this many men." He held up ten fingers over and over again until he did it eighteen times. "This many men!"

Pro nodded and left the masons to tell Zeff the bad news, but Zeff had overheard their conversations. His face had turned a scarlet red. He turned away from Pro and the masons and said over his shoulder, "See, Pro? You see, the gods are against me. You heard him say 'it would take four maybe five summer solstices to do all the work'." Zeff turned to Pro, "That's what he said, I heard him." Zeff pointed at Vor. "The gods are still against me. Pro, you must help me." He grabbed hold of Pro's jacket and pulled him close up. "What can I do? Help me!" Zeff said in a soft voice so the masons would not hear.

Pro looked at the pathetic figure trembling before him. "Look, you have the best masons we can find, and they say it can be fixed and it will be fixed. What more can we do?" Zeff simply walked away. Pro looked at the pitiful man and his memory flashed back to the day in their boyhood when they had climbed to the top of a tall apple tree and Zeff was afraid to come down. The wind blew and the tree swayed back and forth and Zeff broke out into a cold sweat. He clamped himself around the limbs and pleaded with Pro for help. Pro climbed down from the tree, got a rope and ladder and was able to help Zeff come down. Young Pro and Zeff never climbed trees again.

CHAPTER 21   THE ESCAPE

It was late afternoon when Pro joined Jep and the rest of the trading party outside Stonehenge. The campfire had been prepared and everyone was sitting on their haunches in a large circle enjoying the heat from the fire. They all wore gray capes that were draped over their heads and held tightly at the neck for warmth. It looked like a ring of toadstools around the fire. Pro announced, "I don't think Zeff is a danger to us, Jep." Pro smiled broadly. "Zeff is still a little bit affected by the moon, but he and I are still friends like we were when we were young."

"Oh, I thought you were worried that he might attack you." Jep was busy by the fire heating stones in the middle of the coals.

"I was, but it is different now." Pro told the complete story of what had happened at the lintel stone and how Zeff had actually pleaded for help. "The masons will start to build the lintel stone, and we hope Zeff will understand that the stones can't be replaced by the next summer solstice."

Lying on a slab of slate beside the fire were four whole duck carcasses cleaned of feathers, gutted and ready to be roasted. Beside the ducks were many layers of sheep skins soaking in water and a small wool blanket. Jep was busy rolling over various sizes of stones in the fire. Some were the size of a clenched fist and some were half that size, and they were placed on the hottest coals in the fire.

Pro had not paid much attention to what Jep was doing till now. He noticed the ducks and stones and knew exactly what Jep was planning. When the larger stones got hot enough, Jep would put them in the chest cavity of the ducks and place the smaller stones in the cavity under the wings. Then he would wrap the ducks in layers of wet sheep skins and finally wrap them in the wool blanket. In a few hours the ducks would bake and this would provide food for the next two meals. This was a way to eat while on the move without stopping and taking the time to build a fire.

"Jep, why are you preparing food so we can travel? I don't think we need to break up camp and leave today. It's too late in the afternoon to cover any distance."

"I thought you wanted to leave as soon as possible. You thought Zeff was moonstruck and you couldn't trust him." Jep was bent over the fire attending to the cooking.

"Well, I've changed my mind. Besides, if we leave now, we will only have a half day to travel. It's dangerous to travel when it's dark because the night spirits will get us."

"I know, but can't we leave now? I would feel safer if we left." He shooed a fly away from the ducks, then he went to Pro and said, "We gotta leave as soon as we can." He had a worried look on his face and he nodded his head towards one of the people sitting around the fire.

Pro looked at each blanket covered person at the fire. They all looked alike, and he was puzzled. He noticed that there were more in the party now and he counted thirteen. "Wait, we had this many in our trading party," and he held up eight fingers, "and Vor and Una, the masons, that makes this," and he held up ten fingers. Pro started to examine the people individually. Each toadstool had pulled the blanket tightly over their heads and around their necks. All that was visible was two eyes and part of a nose and no one could be recognized. Then Pro peeled back the blanket on one of the toadstools and found a girl with a broad smile with dimples. "It's Dun." Pro dropped to his haunches and sat down beside her. "How are you? By the god of fertility, it's good to see you." He hugged her giving her a gentle squeeze.

"I'm all right but I'm due to have my baby soon." She smiled and glanced at Jep standing off by the fire. "I'm going to have my baby very soon," She swallowed hard and looked down at her swollen belly.

"Pro, be careful," said Jep. "The priests are watching every move we make."

"What do you mean? How did Dun get here?" asked Pro.

"Dun and two other girls escaped while you were looking at the lintel. When Zeff's priests find out they are gone, they will come to get her."

Pro stood up. "Jep is right, we must outsmart them and we must leave, now. Dun, you cover up your head and go pack for Jep. Then, one at a time, I want each of you to get up from the fire and go pack and get ready to leave. Jep, you finish stuffing the ducks and when the ducks are done, we will be ready to go. We will leave by the Icknied Way, but we will only go as far as the Edson stone outcrop. We will cross the river and camp in the woods near the river bank for the night. Hurry now; let's be ready to leave as soon as possible."

Pro's party was out of sight by the time the priests were able to organize a posse. It was dusk when the priests got to the Edson stone outcrop. "Look." One priest pointed to the ground. "Here is a footprint heading that way." He pointed towards the direction of the rising sun. They went off towards the east to the river bank where they stopped and surveyed the shoreline across the river.

"We can't go any further in this dark," said their leader. He looked along the shore line again. "Besides, I think we have lost them."

"But how could they have gone any further in the darkness? It's dense woods over there and you can't even see the trees in front of you in that woods."

"That's true," agreed their leader, and everyone in the party examined the shoreline with more intense scrutiny. The trees and boulders along the shore were easily distinguishable in the illuminating light of the full moon. The bright light also created distinct black shadows, and safely camped in those shadows were Pro and his friends. They had not made a fire and had a roast duck for dinner. They were comfortably nestled in their tents. Except for one guard, one man was lying in the shadows close to Pro's party yet close to the water's edge. He was the sentry, and he could hear every word the priests said as the sound traveled across the river.

"Yes, I think we have lost them. I don't see any light from campfires or smoke in the air. Nothing. Do you see anything?" another priest asked.

"Nothing. Not a thing." The rest of the priests nodded in agreement.

"Let's make camp here before it gets too dark. We'll get an early start and go back to Stonehenge in the morning." The priests made a fire and pitched their tents in a circle. They were all lying around the fire when they heard, "Waa, waa," then a gasp for air and "Waa, waaa" again.

"What's that? Listen." All the priests listened intently but couldn't make out the noise. "Maybe it is a wild night animal."

"No, no, I believe it is one of those ghouls or werewolves or something that come out when the moon is full," moaned a priest.

"Yeah, let's get into our tents and go to bed."

The cry in the night was not a ghoul, a werewolf or a vampire but a healthy baby boy, the first child of Jep and Dun of the Nese clan.

CHAPTER 22 ECLIPSE AT STONEHENGE

Someone from the corner of the crowd called out in a booming voice, "Pro caused the sun to disappear. Kill Pro, kill Pro." Others joined in-- "Kill him! Where's Pro?!"

Pro stood at his tent door listening to the shouting crowd and desperately wondered what to do next. He knew that it would be a matter of minutes before the crowd would determine where his tent was and come after him. For the moment he was protected by the darkness of the eclipse. "Qua, I must do something, they must be made to understand."

"Oh, I'm so afraid, Pro. Pro, what can we do?"   At first Pro didn't answer, then he wrapped his black poncho tightly over his head and started to leave his tent.

"Pro, what are you doing, be careful."

Pro put his finger to his mouth and said, "Shh, shh, I'll be back. I must do something, and this might work."

"Pro, be careful." Qua clung to Pro's poncho holding him back momentarily. "Be careful," she said with tears running down her cheeks.

"Shh. It's our only chance! I'll be back."

"Pro, what are you going to do? Tell me. I want to know." Tears were streaming down her cheeks.

Pro remembered what Wam told him about the eclipse. "Qua, listen," he whispered. "Wam said to me when I was at Avebury that the darkness from eclipses does not last very long. Wam said that the eclipses last as long as it takes for the sun to move from first light to when the full ball appears. That's not very long, and if I can stall the farmers long enough, we'll have sunlight again. I must tell the farmers that before they become violent. I must go!" He held his finger to his lips. "Shh. I'll be back."

"Kill him, get Pro, kill him!" The crowd was stirring about in the dark falling over each other and cursing anyone who got in their way. They were in a state of delirium, half mad with anger and half scared that the sun would never shine again.

Qua held firm to Pro's poncho for one last moment, then said, "I'm so afraid. Do be careful." Her voice trembled and she tried to hide her tears in her handkerchief. Then she released the poncho and Pro pulled it over his face.

"I'll be back," Pro said in a faint unsure voice and he departed with a mock smile and disappeared in the blackness

Pro blindly picked his way through the crowd, careful not to show his face. He almost stepped on someone stretched out on the grass beating and kicking the ground shouting, "The sun, where's the sun?" He stepped around a mother hunched close to a campfire hugging two infant children under her ample shirt, crying. People were moaning and wailing all around Pro as he carefully made his way in the darkness. Finally he reached the heel stone where Zeff was shouting. His poncho was pulled tightly around his head so only his eyes and nose were visible.

"Pro didn't help when he could. He did this to me. We must find him and kill him." Then the high priest's voice went hoarse, he couldn't talk and his face became white. He slipped off the pyramid-shaped heel stone and fell in the arms of his priests. He was a sick man.

"Kill him, get Pro!" Some in the mob were waving their fists in the air and were swinging clubs. "Where's Pro?" The calls were coming from every quarter of the crowd.

Pro had worked his way to the top of the heel stone. His identity was still not known. "Stop!" Pro yelled. There was mass confusion with everyone moaning and milling about. No one was paying attention. "I have something great to tell you, THE SUN WILL SHINE AGAIN," he shouted as loud as he could. "It will shine again. Look!" He pointed to the blackenedout sun, but only a few stopped to listen and look. "Look, look!" Some people made desperate glances at the sun hoping to see daylight, but they were disappointed for it seemed even blacker than before. Pro knew that he must keep talking and hold their attention while not revealing his identity. He glanced down at Zeff on the ground who was still being revived by his priests.

Slivers of light were beginning to shine around the edges of the huge black disk. "The sun will shine again, and we will have the warmth of the sun for our crops. We will again have the light from the sun to see. Look! Everybody look!" Pro screamed. Again he pointed to the sun and more light sparkled and glittered around the edges of the moon. The din of the moaning was slightly less as the people paused to see it there really was more light or whether this was some optical illusion. "It will get brighter and brighter, and soon we shall see all the sun again. Even now it is so bright that you cannot look directly into the light. Look!" Pro had to continue talking and stall for time.

The moaning and wailing began to turn into 'ohs and ahs' of astonishment as the crowd witnessed more sun light. "Look!" Pro shouted. More of the sun was appearing and the crowd began to cheer. Soon louder and stronger rounds of cheers accrued as the crowd realized that the sun was indeed coming back.

The high priest was revived now and recognized that the man under the poncho was Pro. "Pro, you did this to me." He got to his feet and gave Pro a mighty yank on his poncho. Pro reeled to one side and fell five feet to the ground. Then Zeff climbed to the top of the heel stone. "Pro caused the sun to leave us," the high priest shouted. He stood in full height with his arms held high, his albino robe spread in full view. The sun light, although only a shred, accented the white robe and made him look like an eagle ready to take flight.

"He must die," he shouted. "Pro must die."

The crowd was confused, for the sky was still black, but it was gradually getting brighter as more of the sun became visible. Yet the high priest was blaming Pro for the eclipse and yelling for Pro's head.

"Well, let's find Pro and kill him," came a shout from the crowd.

The high priest shouted at the top of his lungs, "He must die. He must di--." He never finished for he was hit hard in the chest with a loud thud. From behind the curtain of blackness a spear had been hurled by someone in the crowd. The spear penetrated deep into the high priest's chest and he fell over backwards and tumbled to the ground. The priests grabbed the spear, trying to pull it out of his chest, but they couldn't.

The crowd's attention was diverted as it became apparent that the sun was definitely going to shine again. They commenced to cheer and shout as smiles appeared on every face.

Pro bent over the high priest. "Zeff?! Zeff!" The scar on his cheek began to tingle and he rubbed it red. He pulled back the albino robe. "Zeff? - Why, you're not Zeff. You're Wam?! Wam from Avebury." Pro was breathless, aghast with shock. "What's going on here? Where is Zeff?" He demanded.

Wam could not answer but only moaned and turned away.

"Where's Zeff? Why is he not here?" Despite Wam's wounded condition, Pro shook him and shouted, "Where's Zeff?"

"I killed him. I had to kill him." Wam was sobbing. "He couldn't handle the high office of chief priest of Stonehenge anymore. I had to kill him so I could make Stonehenge strong again." Then Wam coughed and blood came from his mouth. "I wanted to make Stonehenge respected again."

Pro grabbed Wam by the shoulders. "And Yam, who killed him?.. You killed Yam, didn't you?" Something deep inside Pro told him that Zeff couldn't have committed the murder, not Zeff, not his childhood friend. "You killed Yam out on the trail dressed in Zeff's albino robe, didn't you? You killed him just before I found him. You knew I would be on the trail, didn't you?!"

Wam shook his head. "I had to. We needed the food. He would have ruined it if he told the farmers the simple truth about the eclipse of the sun." Wam made a final gasp for air, coughed and his body went limp. He was dead.

The crowd of worshipers were truly joyous now, singing, cheering, shaking hands, kissing and dancing and making love with the most convenient partner. The crickets stopped chirping and the birds flew back to daylight. The bear keeper even got his bear excited enough to do some tricks.

Pro was oblivious to the merriment as he stared at the dead priest at his feet. He pulled the spear out from Wam's chest and held it in his hand. Who threw this? he thought. "Who saved my life by killing Wam with this?" he wondered. He examined the spear closely. It was old and out of balance, and the flint point was loosely tied down. There were three cross marks carved on the wooden rod. "Whose spear is this, I know I've seen it, but where?"

ABOUT THE AUTHOR

I first visited Stonehenge in 1986 and was disappointed. I commented to my wife at the time that Stonehenge is just a pile of rocks. The clerk at the tourist desk overheard me and gave me some literature to read. Since then I have read practically everything of value on the subject and have found that Stonehenge is a truly fascinating subject. I decided to write and bring life to these wonderful prehistoric people who accomplished so much with so little.

Betrayal at Stonehenge—1000 B.C. takes place at the fall of the Stonehenge epic. The characters in the story are farmers/food producers, and they have a paranoid shaman bound to a strict ritualistic religion. There is a famine, a murder, some love and some loyalty. This is the first of several novels I want to write with Stonehenge as the setting. The book has appeal for the murder mystery fan, the science fiction enthusiast, the religious reader, and those who simply have an intelligent curiosity about the mysteries of Stonehenge.

I am a retired investment banker and live in Shaker Heights, Ohio, with my wife and family nearby.